CTHULHU KAIJU

AHIMSA KERP

SEVERED PRESS
HOBART TASMANIA

CTHULHU KAIJU

PROLOGUE

"They worshipped, so they said, the Great Old Ones who lived ages before there were any men, and who came to the young world out of the sky. Those Old Ones were gone now, inside the earth and under the sea; but their dead bodies had told their secrets in dreams to the first men, who formed a cult which had never died."

H.P. Lovecraft, "The Call of Cthulhu"

A noisome scent overpowered the raw sea air, and Daniel Vigard couldn't stop coughing. Daniel sat aft on his small Zodiac, a cup of coffee in one hand and the sea all around him. The sun climbed from under the mountains behind him, and the only ships that ever came out this early were fishing trawlers and charter boats, neither of which was common this late in the year. He could fit five or six people on his Zodiac, but he knew no one who liked to start their mornings this early, even though it was before the wind started blowing and the sun shone too brightly. It was mid-November, and Daniel had been coming out once a week since June to see the whales.

He often found groups of sea lions, but when he saw whales, it was only their spouts, far off in the distance. The last time he'd seen a whale close up had been early August and now it was close enough to winter that he might not see them again until next summer.

On one hand, he was wasting his time, and he knew it. On the other, he hadn't saved up for most of his adult life to move to the coast, buy a yurt and a boat, and *not* look for whales. The caffeine-infused ritual of waves and gulls and foam and sea was itself enough to live for. On mornings like this, there wasn't another boat within sight, and he felt like old Neptune himself.

Today, however, the smell of something horrible intruded on his happiness. It was a tangible, loathsome scent that clutched at him with cruel talons. For the first time since he was a child, Daniel felt fear. It overrode other concerns and worries, nibbled away at his subconscious.

It was hard to put his finger on what the smell was. Decaying meat, rotting fish, salt and brine; all of these were part of it, but none of them were all of it. Daniel considered himself healthier than most retirees, but this smell sickened him. Not in the disgusted sense of the word, but literally. He could feel ailments assaulting him through the stench; he could feel his body dying. His ex-wife had always said he had a gift for melodrama, but there was no other way to put it.

Below him, a great shadow rose. It was as if a shark were swimming under his boat. Except that in this case the shark was as big as a battleship. Something splashed at the starboard, and out of the corner of his eye he saw a slithering snake. There were no snakes in this part of the ocean. Not on the surface. Not to his knowledge. Uncertainty filled him. This snake, if snake it had been, looked significantly bigger than an anaconda.

Fear blossomed even greater in him, a nameless fear, a fear of dark places, a fear of deep waters. Without making a conscious decision, Daniel turned his Zodiac around.

"Fuck 'em," he muttered, in his great fear dismissing the whales. His heart beat so quickly that he felt he could hear it.

The shadow beneath him grew. It was a somber, royal shade of green that seemed ready to swallow him. Another snake rippled through the waves ahead of him. And then there were snakes all around him, snakes with suction cups, and the stench was so bad, he vomited. His Zodiac was slammed from beneath as something huge hit him, and—.

And there was nothing more for Daniel Vigard ever again.

CHAPTER 1

It says something about the town of Portland, Oregon at the beginning of the 21st century that there were two different bars dedicated to the pulp writer Howard Phillips Lovecraft. The original, simply called 'The Lovecraft Bar,' sat close to the river and had horror-themed nights and goth parties. It does not much come into this story, save for once, much later. The second bar was slightly farther east, between SE Hawthorne and SE Division, and began humbly in a basement. A home-brewing husband and wife served their friends and neighbors ales while someone read from "Call of Cthulhu" or *At the Mountains of Madness*. This second bar quickly grew both in popularity and notoriety, and it expanded to an actual above-ground location within six months. Neither of them, the basement nor the bar, had a sign, but both were known to everyone as Shoggoths. Both of the bars, as much as any business in the city, perfectly fulfilled the local mantra of "Keep Portland Weird."

After the bar opened, the basement fell out of sight, out of mind. There were some stories of hooded figures emerging on moonless nights, whispers of scaled and web-fingered aberrations coming to and fro, reports of men and women entering the house and never being seen again. But this was Portland, a self-proclaimed city of freaks, outcasts, and weirdos, and even when the anecdotes were believed, no one paid them much mind.

***

Maggie stared at her compasses, baffled at their utter failure. Both of them, the red and clear one she'd received from her father on her thirteenth birthday and the newer, much more expensive Brunton, were acting very strangely.

They weren't broken exactly, but it was like they no longer were certain about anything. One moment they trembled achingly in one direction, and the next they inverted their minds and stretched the other way. She adjusted the East/West screws and the North/South, but it was too overcast to use the sun to calibrate them. Besides, the compass arms were jumping around as though on magnetic fire. She didn't have a smartphone, so she radioed the

Hatchery and spoke to Dave.

He attributed it to defective equipment, but he radioed her back a few minutes later, a little breathless. "Damnedest thing," he said. "It's almost as if the poles are shifting, trading places, one minute to the next." Dave had gotten online and told her this phenomenon was already being discussed on message boards for the outdoor inclined. It wasn't just compasses—GPSs were similarly affected.

Maggie gave up on charting the creek, and she drove back to the Hatchery and spent the latter part of the afternoon on the forums, reading about compass failure and describing her own experience. It seemed to be focused in the Pacific Northwest, with most of the chatter coming from Washington, Idaho, and especially the Oregon Coast.

The next morning, as she sipped from a cup of coffee and warmed her hands against the crisp morning air, Maggie got an email. It was sent to her personally, not her work address, and the sender identified only as YOURFRIEND@gmail.com. The message said, rather dramatically: "Seek ye Shoggoths."

Dave was about the age of her father and knew the reference right away. Maggie read mainly nonfiction, but even she had heard the name H.P. Lovecraft. She knew little besides the name, however, and Dave told her about Cthulhu, the octopus-dragon–like creature that slumbered under the sea, and shoggoths, shapeless monsters made of bubbles. It was all a little juvenile, and she didn't understand why so many people were transfixed by a giant octopus.

Maggie ignored the message, but the next day another one came, from the same sender. It read: *Maggie, please listen to me. Great evil is afoot. You need to find the source of it. Go to Shoggoths.*

She didn't use her personal email for anything but staying in contact with friends and family. She marked the message as SPAM and blocked the sender. But the phrase kept tumbling through her mind.

"*Seek ye Shoggoths.*" When she told Dave, he told her about the bar in Portland. "Maybe they mean there?" He had laughed away the idea of a stalker. "You probably linked to something with your name. Or it's someone who knows you in real life. Elena down at

OSU, maybe. I mean, who would stalk you, Maggie?" he asked, not in an unkind way. She liked how he teased her. But he had a point, too.

Maggie's hair was long, always worn in a braid, and she wore a stained bandana when she was out in the field, which was most days. She wasn't fat but knew she was considerably thicker than the women in magazines. She hadn't really dated much at all, not even in college. Men didn't hit on her, and the few times she had initiated, it always backfired. Not that it truly bothered her. Portland and even Hood River was full of pretentious white boys obsessed with the relics of childhood—be it comics, fiction, or windsurfing. They didn't like a dark-skinned girl like her. And the ones that did saw her only for skin, for her heritage. Why was it so hard to find men who saw her for herself?

Maybe her dad was right. He always said she needed to date one of her own kind. He was a disastrous oh-for-three on picking dates for her so far though. And her dad would be the first to admit he was rarely right about anything at all.

The stalker idea didn't really sound plausible, and she had to come into Portland anyway, to pick up the month's supply of chow and pills for Kamuks. He was a mutt through-and-through, mostly black but specked with white spots. He was getting old now, was a little blind in his left eye and not as fleet of foot as he had been, but he was a good pooch. She almost didn't mind the small fortune on his food and heartworm medicine. He rode in the back of her pickup as she cruised the sixty miles along the I-84. There weren't any cops, which was an unexpected bonus.

The shopping trip was uneventful, though Maggie did unexpectedly buy a six-pack of pumpkin beer. After she dropped the heavy bag of food in the back of the truck, patting Kamuks on the head, she cruised around for some time. Southeast Portland was a warren of narrow streets, many claiming to be two-way but with room for only one. There were roundabouts, traffic circles, and plenty of streets that just ended abruptly.

At long last, feeling more stressed than she should, Maggie parked under a tree that had already shed half of its bright yellow leaves. She could see Shoggoths. As Dave had described, it was a signless place between a Bhutanese food cart and a joint that served only pancakes made with microbrews.

"*Seek ye Shoggoths*," Maggie muttered. Her impulse to come to this bar seemed silly now. She didn't go out much, and being around people she didn't know made her feel uncomfortable. But Dave was something of a regular here, and he would ask her about it tomorrow. What could she say? She wouldn't tell him that she was afraid. It was too easy to fall into a rut and do the same things every day.

Decision made, she scratched Kamuks on the chin. "Stay," she told him, leaving him to guard his own food, and crossed the street. Shoggoths was a converted old house, with half a flight of stone steps lit by pumpkin and white star lights leading up to it.

Though it was dark, it was early, not yet seven, and the bar was mostly empty. And still the indolent bartender dismissed her with a glance. In her faded jeans and flannel shirt, she was from Oregon's industrious past and not part of its illustrious future.

She hesitated at the long list of choices—*54 beers on tap* someone had written with pink chalk on a board above the bar. She wavered between ordering a Cthulhu Kaiju Kölsch or a Headless Horseman IPA before ordering a Chocolate Cucumber Stout that she quite enjoyed.

But the clarity she sought was not to be found. No one tried to make eye contact with her, no one came up to speak to her, and she sat there glumly, wondering what she would tell Dave. She didn't feel comfortable ordering another beer and driving home. Drink finished, she paid and left. The night air was chilly for early November, and the darkness had grown. She sighed. It was going to be a long, cold drive back to Hood River. The heater in her pickup had stopped working years ago.

She was halfway across the street when two men grabbed her. She twisted and spun. They were wearing skinny jeans, black jackets, and light green ski masks with several tentacles dangling from the mouth.

"I'a! I'a!" one of them whispered hoarsely at her.

The other pulled his arm back. Something dark and shiny glittered in the streetlight.

Maggie opened her mouth to scream, but a hand clamped down on her as a third man grabbed her from behind. She felt the tentacles from his ski mask whip into her head as she fought back, stomping hard on his foot.

On *her* foot. For a moment, Maggie had had her body pressed against the third attacker and had felt soft breasts pressed into her back. This realization took a moment of Maggie's time, only a scant moment, but it was enough.

The one with the dark metal in his hand brought it down. Maggie twisted so that, instead of her heart, it plunged into her hand. The bright pain slashed through her body and her mind reeled. Blood spurted out; far too much blood, far too quickly.

Now she screamed. The three closed in on her, blood leaking from the hard blade onto the dark street. They pressed in on her, and she felt more hopeless than she ever had.   The blade was in the air again, and she realized it was volcanic, an obsidian dagger.

The dagger clattered to the ground as a savage shape hit the knife-wielder. Kamuks leaped in front of Maggie protectively and growled in a way that Maggie had never heard. It was a primal protective growl, the kind that brooked no dissent.

Faced with a fanged guard instead of an unsuspecting victim, the three ski-masked assailants fled into the dark night. Maggie stumbled to the sidewalk and slumped to the ground, afraid to look at the deep cut.

A young woman with blue hair dropped her bike to the ground and ran to her. "Are you alright? I saw you, but I thought you were filming a movie or something."

"I'm fine," Maggie said with effort.

"Let me call the cops."

"Don't do that," Maggie said. "My dog. He bit them."

"He was defending you," the blue-haired girl said.

"Do you think that will matter to them? I'll be fine. Really. Thanks for your concern."

The girl stared at her as she climbed back into her pickup, Kamuks in the passenger seat now. Maggie drove out of the city and back toward home. An old shirt staunched the blood, but the pain and the aching only grew.

She didn't want to deal with the police, but she did need a doctor. Health insurance was expensive, and she had opted out, gambling on her good health so she could save for grad school. At any rate, she could clean and bandage the wound herself tonight and deal with it tomorrow.

Maggie suddenly pulled her truck over and leaped out into the darkness. Kamuks whined plaintively at her, but she hardly heard him. She vomited into the bushes as the reality of the attack finally set in. Her body trembled irrationally, and the old cloth wrapped around her hand was soaked through.

She looked up at the night sky and forgot the attack, the throbbing in her hand, forgot everything. It was dark on the road from Portland to the Gorge; the shadows were awash in starlight. But they were the wrong constellations. She was looking at the wrong galaxy. The stars were wrong.

CHAPTER 2

"What is that smell?" Anna asked. Her nostrils flared as she scanned the beach for any possible culprits. But there was nothing that seemed out of the ordinary. No obvious collections of garbage or boats filled with rotting fish.

"*Noe lukter vondt*," Cato said. He wore black-rimmed glasses and skinny jeans.

"Um, in English, please," Carter asked.

"Something smells terrible," Anna translated. Her gaze turned to the sea. "Look at that cloud. Is that usual here?"

Carter looked. The cloud in question was ominously hovering over the sea, alone in the blue vastness. It was colored a sickly green, like someone had vomited pea soup.

"I haven't ever seen anything like it," Carter said. "It kind of creeps me out."

"We don't have such clouds in Norway," Cato said.

"We don't normally have them here," Carter replied. "Maybe it's that cloud that stinks. Some kind of gas accumulation?"

"I don't think it's the cloud I smell," Anna said. "Come on."

"I don't want to get in the way of your couple time," Carter said. "Three's a crowd."

"We're not a couple," Cato said. Anna just laughed. People always thought that. Didn't they realize that most people spent more time with coworkers and friends than they did with their partners? The probability did not line up.

"Why does everyone here think that?" she asked, shaking her head. It seemed a silly assumption. "I just don't get it. Anyway, let's get to exploring the beach."

Cato followed her, as he always did. They were coworkers from Scancom, a small technology firm in Oslo. The two were in Oregon for a week researching a new type of desalination that promised to change the world. That was the official purpose of their trip, at any rate.

After working through jetlag in the Portland office for four long fourteen-hour days, they were going to the beach for the day. Their

American liaison, Carter, who worked for an affiliate company, had offered to drive them. Both had accepted, though each would have rather gone rock climbing or downhill biking or done something more active.

They had slept in that morning and driven out from Portland to a small town called Seaside. It was a significant tourist attraction in the summer, but on this cool autumn weekday the beach was nearly empty. A couple walked hand in hand, leaving footprints in the wet sand. A toddler threw a stick for a dog while his parents beamed and took dozens of pictures. A young woman sat in the grass and sketched. Apart from them, the beach was deserted.

The smell grew worse as they walked south. After half an hour, they saw the gulls, hundreds of them. Thousands of them. The white birds were swarming over the sand and landing in the shallow waves. Cato gagged and had to pull his shirt up to breathe.

"Is that what I think it is?" Carter asked.

"I think so," Anna answered. "Come on."

The shrieks of the gulls as they fled before the human interlopers were nigh deafening. Their flight revealed a twisted sight. Thousands of dead sea creatures were washing ashore—fish mainly, but also seals, octopuses, even a few massive sea lions. More were brought in with the fresh waves even as they watched.

"*Faen*," Cato swore through his shirt. "We should go now."

"I'm with you, man," Carter said. "We can call the cops and let them figure it out."

"Look at that," Anna said, pointing at something far bigger than a sea lion. Her face showed no sign of discomfort. She lived for this kind of stuff. In school, her friends had said she was morbid. She preferred to think of it as having curiosity, but there was no denying that she had to stop herself from smiling. She pulled out her phone and took several pictures.

The putrid green cloud quickly drew nearer to them, but they did not notice. All of them were staring at the fourteen-meter-long dead whale that had just washed up. It was dark skinned, covered in gray patches and white mottling. More seagulls flew overhead. Some few dared to land on the far side of the fish graveyard and peck at the flesh buffet.

"A gray whale," Cato said. "The Atlantic Ocean pods are

extinct, and I've never seen one before. They are a cool animal. And they have a good nickname, too," he added, his voice a little quiet.

"What is it?" Anna asked. It was Carter who answered her.

"They call them the Devil Fish," he said. Cato nodded in affirmation. "We get whales washing up here every so often. There's actually a skeleton of one at the aquarium. This is bad, though. Not natural at all. Radiation from Fukushima, maybe?" At that thought, he pulled out his phone and called the office.

Anna turned to Cato. The whale, even dead, was an awesome sight. Even though two meters of it were up on the dry sand, its massive body stretched back into the ocean for longer than they could see.

"What is coming out of its face? I've never seen anything like it," Anna said.

Cato stared. Long gray tentacles, the underside of which were pinkish white, stretched from the animal's mouth. Perhaps they bobbed in the ocean water, but it seemed that they were still moving. It was hard to say with certainty, but the tentacles appeared to be growing naturally from the whale's body.

Squawking gulls descended as more dead sea life washed ashore. The wind picked up, blowing sand in their faces and chilling them. The rotting corpse smell was more pungent than ever.

"It must have eaten an octopus or something," Cato said. "And the tentacles got attached somehow to its face." The explanation didn't sound reasonable even to him.

Carter hung up. "They didn't hear anything about Fukushima. That's one relief, I guess. But that cloud is almost on us, and I don't like the look of it. We don't have rain jackets, either. Let's go back."

"Maybe someone will come pick us up," Anna said.

"In your dreams!" Carter said. Cato liked this expression. It seemed so American to him.

"Just let me take a few more pictures," Anna said. She was the kind of girl men didn't usually say no to, and neither did now. Cato pulled a small digital camera from his bum bag and took a few photos as well. It was certainly ground zero for *something*, and he shared, to a lesser extent, Anna's excitement at being the first witnesses there. As they watched, the whale sluggishly came more onto the shore, sliding upon the wet sand.

"Um, guys?" Carter said. "Look up."

The tenebrous cloud had reached them. It lurked over their heads, glowing with unhealthy radiant energy.

"This is not good," Carter said.

Anna took a photo of it. Rain fell down, glowing green drops that sizzled. They hit the whale's carcass, and there was a creaking, stretching sound.

"*Faen!*" Cato cried.

"Watch your language," Anna said. He cursed too much, especially knowing that no one around them could understand him.

The whale's flesh and the bodies of the sea life stretched and cracked where the rain hit them. They were *drying*, as though being instantly mummified. It was a gruesome sight, seeing the freshly dead animals instantly dehydrate. Far worse was realizing the same fate awaited them.

"I don't want that shit to touch me," Carter said. Even as he spoke, a sparkling drop the color of fresh bile hit his jacket sleeve. It immediately dried like paper. Carter screamed. Around them gulls were dying in droves, screaming their pain as the rain sucked all moisture from them.

"The rain," Anna said. "It's going to kill us!"

"Under the whale," Cato said. "It's our only hope."

The drops fell heavier. Over their heads, the cloud didn't look so small after all. It robbed the sky of all else.

"Are you guys crazy?" Carter asked. "Under the whale?"

"It's a dreadful idea," Anna said. "But we have to try it."

She scurried forward. A drop hit her hair, and she felt it stiffen as though it had been blow-dried for hours. That terrified her.

She dove into about two feet of seawater and slid under the whale. Seconds later Cato joined her. Its body was buoyed up as the tide came in. It didn't leave much space, but it was enough. The drying rain became a monsoon, the animal carcasses withered, and the sea itself retreated from the shriveling touch of the rain.

"Where's Carter?" Anna asked. Cato's ear was close to her mouth, but she had to yell to be heard over the stretching sound of dead flesh and the cacophony of shrieking birds. They both shivered in the cold ocean water. Cato took off his glasses, which had steamed up in their small space. Above them, the whale settled and shifted down. They now had less than ten centimeters of breathing room.

"I can't see him," Cato said. "I think he ran the other way."

"*Faen*," Anna said.

It was a nightmarish wait, their bodies freezing as they lay between the ever-crushing whale and the evaporating seawater. Fish corpses bobbed in the water and hit them in the face. Worst were the lobsters, whose sharp claws stuck like an unheeded warning. But as nightmares do, it ended suddenly. It was over. The birds stopped screaming, the ocean water ceased receding, and the spectral cloud fled inland, across the forests of fir, to the east. Cato and Anna climbed out from under the whale, shaking from cold but laughing from relief that they were alive. But that relief quickly dissipated as they walked down the beach

They found Carter's desiccated body less than ten meters away. He hadn't run nearly far or fast enough.

CHAPTER 3

She walks alone, the paved highway beside her. It is empty. SHIFT She is in an airplane, and beneath her is a wide stretch of sea. SHIFT Now it's a river. She stands on a bridge, looking at the water below her. The water is blue, the river is cold, this she knows. But something is wrong. SHIFT She lies on the bridge, the cold, rusting green metal pressed into her cheek, into her body. She scarcely feels it. Her gaze is held fast by the river.

The water is full of fish. Dead fish. Dead fish filling the water until there is no river at all, merely a channel of bloated corpses flowing toward the sea. There are so many salmon and trout and sturgeon and steelhead and walleyes and other, stranger, larger fish, too. Fish from the deep depths of the sea, fish with iridescent scales, and fish with no scales at all. Some have yellow eyes and others sport tiny vestigial arms or legs.

They rise out of the water, pushing ever higher, rise up as though being pushed by underwater gears. They climb the sky. Each of the fish, common and exotic, stares at her with vacant, accusatory eyes. Maggie is alone in the world, save for the piles of fish that fill the sky in sloppy, rubbery pyramids all around her. The bridge begins to sink.

***

"You were what?"

"I was attacked," she repeated. Her voice was dry and matter-of-fact, as though she were talking about someone else. "Three men. In the street. Well, two men and a woman."

"A woman! You can't trust these people, Magpie," her father said. "Something about living so close together makes people crazy in the head." Her father thought of Hood River, a town of 8000 people, as too big for anyone to actually want to live there. His own house was only a few miles from the city, but those miles seemed to make all the difference for him. It was a familiar refrain, a mantra that she had grown up with. Now, for the first time since she was a child, she wondered if it was true.

She sat next to her dad, she on a foldable cloth picnic chair and he in his wicker rocking chair. From his porch, they looked down

14

onto the Columbia Gorge. The view was spectacular. Some days she hardly noticed it at all—the mundaning of the familiar—but today that gray sliver of the Columbia River, sliding through the verdant valley flanked by rocky cliff walls, seemed as beautiful as anything could be.

It was chilly out on the porch, her nose and cheeks reddened in the wind, but the view was worth it. The fresh air was worth it. The peace of mind wrought by nature and her father's presence was worth it.

"So it's my fault again?" Maggie asked. This was familiar territory for the both of them. "I go into the city, and I deserve whatever happens to me?"

"That's not what I meant," Leonard said. He frowned, searching for the words. "It's just—it's hard on a father when he can't protect his daughter. You're all I have."

"I know. That's why I came to you."

He smiled. "Not calling the police was the right idea," he said. "They'll never take the word of our kind over white folk."

"They were wearing masks, Dad. We don't exactly know they were white," she pointed out.

He stopped rocking in the chair and leaned up. "They were wearing Cthulhu ski masks," he said. "Sounds pretty goddamned white to me."

"You know who Cthulhu is?" She couldn't hide her surprise.

"Hey, I might be an old man, but I'm an old man who knows his South Park," her dad said, a familiar twinkle in his eye. "Now let's get inside and call Dr. Canfield. Your fingers are turning blue out here."

***

"You were what?" Dave from work had initially thought she was kidding. Not until Maggie showed him the bandaged wound did he believe her. "In Portland? Southeast Portland? Not Gresham?"

"Just outside the bar," she said. Maggie had taken the morning off to visit her father and to get her wound cleaned and treated. Fridays at the Hatchery were typically slow, anyway, and she had arrived with a bagful of burritos from the local taco shop.

"You're okay, though? I feel awful. I encouraged you, didn't I?"

"It's not your fault, Dave."

"I wish I hadn't done it," he said, shaking his graying head solemnly.

"I'm fine, really. I'm more surprised than anything. Who would do such a thing?"

"Meth heads," Dave answered. Everyone who lived in the Gorge, or indeed who had ever parked at a trailhead in the Gorge, had had their vehicle broken into. Say one thing: meth heads were many things, but discriminatory was not one of them. They robbed from rich and poor with equal gusto. Maggie had even had the tape player stolen out of her pickup.

Maggie shook her head. "I don't think so." She told Dave about the strange knife, about the tentacle masks, and as an afterthought added the words one of them had whispered. She didn't tell him about the stars, just as she had not told her father. That clearly had been a result of stress and pain. Surely there had been nothing wrong with the night sky.

Dave's eyes grew big, and he put down his foil-wrapped rice-and-bean burrito. "Are you screwing with me?"

"No. What? Why would I?"

"It just sounds like your classic case of Cthulhu cultists is all. But the Lovecraft festival was last month. And I don't think any of them would actually stab you." He picked up his burrito and took another bite. A little bit of avocado squished out and fell onto his desk. "What did the police say?"

She hesitated, not sure what to say.

"Oh that's right, you don't believe in police." His grin belied the words. "You always do this. I remember when we did Habitat for Humanity, and you dropped the board on your foot. You wouldn't let any of us take you to the hospital, either."

"I don't like doctors," Maggie said. The subject always made her uncomfortable. She accepted everyone else's weirdness. Why couldn't they accept hers?

"Maggie, your big toe was broken."

"Sure. I didn't know that, though."

"A doctor would have." Dave sighed. "No problem, no problem. It doesn't mean we can't do some Nancy Drewing ourselves." He paused for a moment in thought. "From what you said, those masks are the ones they sell in half a dozen Etsy shops. Hell, I think I saw some down at Saturday Market. But that knife. There can't be too many obsidian blades around. I will do some research. Make some calls."

"Thanks, Dave," she said. "It means a lot." She didn't expect much in the way of results from him, but the support it symbolized reassured her. She'd been bullied so much as a child that it sometimes surprised her when people were genuinely kind.

Maggie sat down at her desk, filled with a strange listlessness. It was already two. There really wasn't enough time to start any new projects. Seven new emails waited for her. One was from "YOURFRIEND."

She deleted it, unread. Whatever games were going on, she did not want any part of it. She still didn't have any answers as to why her compasses had become unstable, but that mystery no longer seemed so tantalizing. She had been planning a hike up Eagle Creek this weekend, but staying in with her pooch sounded much cozier.

The phone on her desk rang. She picked it up slowly.

"Hello?"

"Maggie, you have to listen to me," an intense voice said.

"Who is this?"

"A friend. Sorry about last night. The Accursed moved faster than I had planned on."

Maggie almost dropped the phone receiver. "How did you get this number? Who are you?"

"That's not important. But I think I can trust you. I can't trust anyone else, but I can trust you. You have to listen. I know why the GPS isn't working. Why the poles don't mean anything. Why there are volcanoes erupting and earthquakes queueing up across the world."

"Were you behind what happened? Were you there last night?" Unknowingly, her face had twisted in disgust.

"I was in the bar, but you were followed in. I saw you there, but I couldn't talk to you. They were watching."

"Don't ever call me again," she said.

"Don't hang up! The compasses aren't working because the continents are coming back together. The return of Pangaea. It will happen soon, within a month or two."

"That's impossible," she snapped.

"Not for him. He wants it back. Like it was."

"Like it was when? And who are you talking about?"

"Like it was when he was last awake. Two hundred million years ago." The caller left Maggie's other question unanswered.

CHAPTER 4

It was already late in the afternoon on a soggy Friday when Wasp parked his motorcycle and grabbed an order of fish and chips. The fish was old and the chips undercooked, but he wolfed it down dry in under two minutes. Only then did he pour the tartar sauce into his mouth. It mixed with half-chewed pieces of potatoes and a chunk of halibut stuck in his teeth. The young waitress was openly staring at him. Wasp was used to it. He was a big guy, with slicked-back hair, a leather vest, and enough tattoos and scars to stand out even sans strange culinary rituals. Especially in the places he'd been traveling. He burped loudly, once, paid, and crossed the street.

This was the real reason he had stopped here, in this town that hadn't changed much since the last time he'd been here. And that had been in the eighties. A man and a woman stood smoking in front of the front door, between the Budweiser and Keno neons.

"Hold up, buddy. You can't come in here," the man said. He held out his hand, right in front of Wasp's chest.

Wasp stared at the man, a leather jacket–clad biker. The instinct to look menacing warred in Wasp with genuine surprise. It was rare for a ramshackle bar such as this to have a bouncer, particularly this early in the day. They were lucky he was such a chill guy.

The blonde woman next to him grabbed the bouncer's bicep with both her hands. "Tyler, shut the fuck up."

To Wasp, she said, "Come on in, sir. Have a Pendleton on the house."

Wasp nodded once. Respect. That was more like it. She even knew the kind of bourbon he drank.

As he entered the club, he heard the woman say to the man in hushed tones, "Don't you know who that is?"

Wasp didn't hear the man's reply. But it didn't matter. If they knew who he was, if they remembered, this would be much easier.

The bar was like any small town bar. Full of lowlifes, white trash, and junkies. Light beer on draft. Jukebox stocked with Foreigner, Boston, and Alabama. Wasp relaxed just a little. It was his kind of place. It was his kind of people.

He sat down at an unoccupied table, and the waitress brought him a double. He sipped it and looked around the bar. He realized that everyone in there must be part of the Brotherhood, which explained the bouncer at the door. Most of them were young, new faces to him, but he thought he recognized a few old-timers. They had been around in '79/'80 when he had pulled off the St. Helens gig.

The seventies had been a good time for the Brotherhood, especially in Oregon. With a volcano within a hundred miles of two major cities, Wasp had used the power of his most sacred possession to cause the eruption. It had been spectacular, but until very recently the St. Helens achievement had been seen as a debacle. Nothing had happened. *He* had not awoken. The Brotherhood disbanded, and the members went on to become the dregs of society: alcoholics, inmates, junkies, and stockbrokers.

Wasp lost his position and almost his life. No one would listen to him—"*These things take time, hombre*" became his mantra. Ousted, he had left the country for good (or so he had thought at the time) and ridden his bike all the way down to Peru. It had been good down there, but when scientists recorded the Bloop, Wasp knew he had unfinished business in Oregon. The Bloop—a song from R'lyeh sent across the oceans. But it had been confirmed just two weeks ago, when that call came in. The eruption *had* been enough to wake *him*, although thirty-five human years passed before anyone knew that. Thirty-odd years—most of his life, and all of his good years. But less than a blink for *him*.

And now vindication time had come. With Wasp's leadership, humanity didn't have to be completely wiped out. Just enough to restore balance to the world. And make the big guy happy. A few billion might go, but all things considered, everyone else would be better off.

"Look at him. He's out of it," a deep voice said. Wasp looked up to see a muscled young man with a sharp face and a bristly goatee standing in front of him. Flanking him were a few seedy-looking men, including the bouncer who had tried to stop him and a tall skinny man still wearing his motorcycle helmet.

"You should choose your words with more care, hombre. I

am—"

"I know who you are! Or should I say: I know who you were. Times change."

"Be careful, Luther," one of the older women cautioned. "Wasp don't fuck around."

"Yeah, well, I don't, either."

The expression on Wasp's face didn't change at all. He hadn't really expected a challenge here, among his people. But he'd been gone too long, and the young tigers had grown used to their domain. They did not welcome the return of their true master.

"I was invited here as a guest," Wasp said.

"I invited you, fool!" Luther said. "One more loose end I have to take care of." There was something in his stance that suggested military training to Wasp.

Wasp leaned back casually in his chair. "I don't have to tell you where this stone comes from, do I?" He reached up and found the kelp cord around his neck. The strange angles and humming from the stone made it obvious, even if the man hadn't previously known. The rock of R'lyeh, the power that had caused the eruption of St. Helens. And that was not all it could do. "I don't have to tell you the power that it gives me. Now fuck off, before I have to hurt you." He downed his bourbon and burped again, tasting a mélange of fish, tartar sauce, and whiskey.

"That's real pretty," the young man said. His tone was sneering, though his face remained a study in passivity. Wasp frowned. Surely they weren't going to make him go through with it.

Luther ran his right hand through his hair. His left hand disappeared into his black windbreaker. Everyone in the bar was watching them. The air crackled with the energy that appeared only when a fight was about the happen. Wasp didn't feel he had many options left.

"Are you going to bark all day, little doggy?" Wasp asked, quoting one of his favorite films. Sheer bravado was usually all it took to establish dominance.

"It just so happens," Luther said. "I'm going to bite." His left hand came out from his jacket. Resting in his palm was a pulsing stone with the angles all wrong. It didn't look exactly like Wasp's, but it was close enough. Besides, there was no way to fake a rock of R'lyeh.

"But how!" Wasp said, unable to hide his surprise. "I am the Accursed. The Sacred Stone is mine."

"You were gone too long, old man. And you were never good enough. *He* wants me to lead now. I am the Accursed."

"Are you challenging me?" Wasp asked. His voice was filled with quiet menace. He guessed now at the identity of the creature wearing the motorcycle helmet. "You meddle with forces you do not understand. They will destroy you."

Luther paused. "I will challenge you, and I will kill you. Or you can just give me the rock and go away. Leave this place and never come back." His face had yet to betray the slightest emotion. He sounded bored.

Wasp stood up abruptly, his wooden chair falling to the cold ground.

The people in the bar who had any idea at all of what was going on, and there were more than a few, started running. They ran to their cars and bikes, sped off onto the highway without looking back, and drove down to California or up to Washington or across the state to Idaho.

That left a few ignorant and morbidly curious remaining to see the showdown as the two Accursed faced off. The tall man in the motorcycle helmet fearlessly watched the battle.

A minute later, the entire seaside town was engulfed in flames.

CHAPTER 5

Saturday morning arrived and with it came the sun. It was impossible to resist a rare blue sky, and Maggie decided to go for a hike after all. She loaded up her day bag and grabbed the leash for Kamuks. On cold days when they were alone, she would often let him off leash on the trail, where he would disappear for hours. He always returned to her, no matter if she had turned around or taken another trail. It had worried her when he was still a puppy, but she had long since accepted Kamuks's preternatural homing instincts.

On the way, she stopped at Cascade Locks for gas and coffee. It was a small town, even by Gorge standards, and she knew it well. Her dad had taken her through here at least once a month on their excursions up into Washington. The claim to fame of this small town was the grandiloquently named Bridge of the Gods.

This bridge connected Washington and Oregon, which were separated here by about seven hundred feet of river. The bridge always brought to mind one of her favorite stories as a child. The chief of all gods, Tyhee Saghalie, and his two sons, Klickitat and Wy'east, had come down from the far north looking for a new home. When they found eastern Oregon, they all naturally decided it was the most beautiful land they had ever seen. In fact, Klickitat and Wy'east, who had been best of friends, quarreled over ownership of the land. When gods quarrel, it's a very serious business. Both were powerful, and neither could gain the upper hand.

At last their father wearied of their struggle and took his mighty bow and shot two arrows. One he aimed north, in the direction they had traveled down from. Klickitat obligingly packed up and traveled north. The other arrow went south, into terra incognita, and Wy'east went to settle where that arrow had landed.

The wily Tyhee Saghalie had acquired the prized land for himself, a fact both of his sons became aware of all too late. The two brothers patched up their friendship. In order for them to meet, they built the original Bridge of the Gods, one made of earth and stone rather than steel. That natural bridge had eventually been washed away in a flood, and years later men built the metal one, and the name remained.

When she walked out of the gas station, coffee in hand, a green VW was parked next to her car, and two young men were loitering by her truck. Maggie fought the impulse to flee and walked up to them. Before she said anything, one of them spoke.

"Seek ye Shoggoths," the taller of the two said. He was strikingly thin and had a tan that had obviously been acquired out of state. His eyes were intense, and his voice was all too familiar. "I think a proper introduction is due at this point, Maggie."

The man next to him, rounder though still thin, wearing glasses and a nervous smile, added, "We're friends, promise. We want to help stop all this."

"All what? Why are you bothering me?"

"At this point, you're involved because you're involved. The Accursed is looking for you," the beanpole said.

"I'm Arlo," said the less intense one. "My friend here is Orson. We stumbled onto this about the same time you did."

"We could use a friend," Orson said. "They are hunting us, too."

It all felt so ridiculous. Maggie almost told them to fuck off. But she remembered the helpless feeling when she had been surrounded. There had been something harrowing about those attackers. She did not sense that here. She walked over to her truck and patted Kamuks in the back. He panted at her happily, but she thought she could sense his impatience.

"You're the one who messaged me." She sipped at her coffee. It was still way too hot to drink.

Orson nodded.

"And called me."

He nodded again.

"Tell me about the plates coming back together," she said. "Where did that come from?"

"It's hard to explain," Arlo said. "But I believe Orson. He's done a lot of traveling."

Maggie frowned. "I'm going to need more than that."

"Word. There is some scholarship about it, even though it might be in the 'kook' category," Orson said.

"It's definitely in the 'kook' category," Arlo amended.

"Yeah, okay. They called it Amasia, a super continent made when the Arctic Ocean holds a party that the Americans and Asians both drive up northward to attend. Of course, this could do things like close off the Arctic Sea, destroy the Atlantic and Indian oceans, and merge all the continents back together. The thing is, it's all theoretical. And even in theory it shouldn't happen for a hundred million years yet."

"And that's happening now?"

"Indeed," Orson said. "But the good news is we'll be dead or enslaved long before it happens."

Maggie frowned.

"There's a lot more to tell you," Arlo interjected. "But maybe out here in the parking lot isn't the best place to do it." She noticed that several people were watching them with dull-eyed hostility. Well, it was a small town. A little bit of hostile curiosity was not surprising.

Arlo asked her about places they could go while Orson pulled his phone out of his pocket and stared at the screen. He was absorbed for several moments, so much so that he didn't notice Arlo or Maggie coming closer to him. When he looked up, his face was pale.

"I don't know what this means, but it's bad."

"What happened?" Arlo asked.

"It's started already."

He turned his phone out and pressed play on a video.

Maggie had to stare for a few moments. It was a small coastal town, and it was on fire, with heavy smoke obscuring the camera's view. In the distance, it looked as though a giant, humanoid orca was fighting an enormous, equally humanoid lobster. It looked like a low-budget Godzilla movie, except with no Godzilla.

"What am I watching?" she asked. "A Godzilla movie without Godzilla?" They did not hear her.

"That's not *him*," Arlo said.

"No, Cthulhu has not returned yet. These may be lieutenants, other creatures trapped in R'lyeh that no record exists of."

"What?" Maggie asked. But just then Kamuks barked loudly. Maggie looked up in alarm.

None of the watchers in the town had drawn closer, or moved

toward them at all. In fact, now she wondered whether they had been watching her at all. Was she getting paranoid?

"What's wrong, boy?" she asked the dog. He was whining now, plaintively, as though he were really hungry. She suspected he was impatient that they weren't already on the trail.

It took her a few seconds to realize the ground was shaking. Oh hell, Maggie thought. Portland and all of western Oregon was on the Cascadia fault, a fault line that rivaled the more famous San Andreas and was long overdue for a major quake.

The shaking grew worse, and Maggie clutched the side of her truck for stability.

"We've got company," Orson said.

A trio of people on motorcycles veered off the road and came throttling toward the three of them.

"Get in the truck," Maggie said. "Hurry."

Before she could take a step, a strong tremor threw her to the ground. Maggie picked herself up and saw the riders jump from their bikes, which crashed to the paved parking lot, wheels spinning.

The riders kept their feet, and one, she saw, had something black and shiny in his hands. The newcomers' faces were obscured by the motorcycle helmets, but Maggie suddenly feared they were the same trio from outside of Shoggoths.

Maggie jumped up and flung her mostly full coffee cup at the chest of one of the riders. She never saw if it hit. The earth reeled once more, as if drunk, and Maggie was hurled against the truck. She saw Orson and Arlo flailing to stay upright. The motorcycle riders were joined by a handful of townsfolk. So it hadn't been paranoia, not completely, anyway. Maggie was trembling. She bit her lip as a helmeted rider advanced upon her, a dark obsidian blade held tightly in his fist. He came toward her across the trembling earth.

Orson and Arlo moved in front of her. Fists swung. Heads cracked. And barking filled the air, but she had tied Kamuks up too well. This time he couldn't save her. Another tremble knocked everyone to the ground. She stood again unsteadily, staring at the blue sky. What was happening? Someone slapped her. Orson had a bloody nose and bruises on his face. He was screaming at her, she realized. Had been for some time. The motorcycle riders and their townie friends were still picking themselves up. Arlo too was still on the ground, blood leaking from his scalp.

"Give me your keys!" Orson said, not for the first time, but she held onto them, and Maggie and her new friends scrambled into the truck, just ahead of their attackers. The next thing she knew, they were in her truck, all three of them piled in the cab, and she was reversing. The ground continued to shake, and there was a dreadful wrenching, scraping sound. The riders ran for their bikes, but she was free and on the road, riding away through the bucking quake.

"This is insane!" she shouted, relief at being alive overriding all else.

"Get used to it," Orson said darkly. "Insanity is going to become a lot more normal."

They sped away from Cascade Locks. The shaking continued; buildings collapsed and trees tumbled. The Bridge of the Gods itself at last fell into the Columbia River with a groan and a sigh.

CHAPTER 6

The town of Cannon Beach on the Oregon coast no longer existed. The smoking ruins left by the battle of the two titans had been rapidly submerged by the following tsunami. Two different catastrophes in one day, and either would have been sufficiently destructive on its own. The one silver lining was that few people had died. Most of the locals lived prepared for tsunamis and had escaped the town even with short notice. The army reserves arrived within hours, and they had been followed by elite governmental forces not long after. It took those in charge, the governor and the army colonels, some time to realize what anyone could have seen at first sight.

Humanity had lost this battle, almost before it had begun. Although stories of giant monsters were told by wild-eyed witnesses, they were dismissed by even the most credulous. There were real problems to focus on. The destruction of the earthquake and the resulting tsunamis spread from Tillamook all the way up past Seaside. Tales each more unbelievable than the last circulated quickly through the beachside communities and onto the net.

Anna and Cato were still in shock over the death of Carter. They had been rescued from the beach mere minutes before the cascading waves had crushed the city. Now they sat with other rescued townspeople, a few miles inland, under a blue tarp that dripped with rain. A volunteer handed them steaming mugs of coffee.

"I want to go home," Anna said.

Cato stared at her, unsure of what to say. The statement was so unlike her.

"I want to, but I won't," she said. "There is something entirely new here, something unknown. What we learn here could help Scancom."

Cato sighed. He should have known. "The Ragnarök?" he asked. "You're thinking about that now? Our trip was supposed to be a break from that."

"A break? We brought a prototype with us, Cato. If we can make the R99, Scancom will be insanely successful. We can retire.

Besides, it is our duty as scientists to see what happens," she said.

"What if we die?" he asked quietly. The rain splattered overhead on the tarp.

She shrugged. "We will die someday, anyway. Besides, there are worse things than death."

He didn't point out that those worse things were confronting them now. She was well aware of that, having seen the whale's body and what happened to Carter. But she was right, too. He couldn't leave now. Not without more information. Even miserable and cold and frightened, his mind was spinning with questions. What did it all mean? Above all, the idea of field-testing the Ragnarök did appeal to him.

The hubbub of people around them suddenly increased with excitement. Cato heard mentions of the Air National Guard, the Navy, and something called NORAD. The Americans were not sure what they were fighting against, but, dammit, they were sure they would fight back with all they had. Typical Americans. They were like the barking little dogs that everyone here had. Cato smiled at the thought.

The ground shook, creaking with an enormous tremor. Everyone went silent. Aftershocks could be nearly as big as a quake. A few seconds later, the ground rumbled. The jumbo coffee pot half full of steaming brew went crashing to the ground and shattered. The ground continued to pulse every couple seconds, but each time it was less extreme and seemed farther away. At last, the shaking diminished entirely, leaving the refugees together with nothing but a sense of far-away foreboding.

Anna's eyes were big. "Do you know what that sounded like?"

Cato shook his head.

Her voice was so low that she almost whispered. "Footsteps."

***

They slept in a motel in a small town about forty kilometers inland that night. The motel was full, and they shared a small room. Small by American standards, which were on a different scale entirely from Norwegian. They were happy to be warm and dry and safe. After watching reruns of *Gloom* and eating burritos as big as their heads, they both passed out. Cato's dreams were awful, haunting.

He was under the sea, and around him was only darkness. In the dream, he could breathe and walk underwater with no problem. There was something he was looking for. But with each step he took, he grew smaller. The darkness surrounded him, clutched at him with icy tendrils, and *something* loomed above him.

The dream shifted, and he was back in Oslo. He was riding his bike to work, except that his bike wasn't really a bike. It was a horse. And all the people around him were staring at him. Their eyes were filled with menace. He couldn't escape the thought that they meant to hurt him, to chew on him and bite him and drink his blood. Then, Cato realized they weren't really people at all; they were hounds, people-sized hounds, and even as he knew this, the beasts began to lope after him.

His horse was a motorcycle now, and he gunned it. He took off, flying down the streets, which now were country roads, farms stretching on either side of him. But the hounds were behind him, growing closer. They were as tall as people, their bodies lean with hunger, and their jaws slavered with green froth.

The same green was in the sky, haunting the clouds. Around him it began to rain, and Cato knew this was no normal rain but that abhorrent unrain. It hit his face, and he was not on a motorcycle anymore, nor in Norway, but back on that beach, and death was all around him, in all the angles of the world. He screamed and screamed.

***

Anna woke him up, shaking him. Even disoriented, even shaking, he could see the tears on her face.

"What's wrong?" he asked her. "Are you okay?"

She smiled. "I want to ask you that. You are the one screaming."

Cato sat up. A blurred sense of terror filled him. "Yes. I was dreaming. We were back at the beach." Saying that, he knew there had been more, and it felt important to remember, but even as he grasped for it, the remains of the dream evaporated forever.

"I dreamed, too," Anna said. "I think there were wolves. Tall skinny wolves that chased me across the world."

Cato shivered without knowing why. He stood up, putting on his glasses and a tee shirt. "I should have expected nightmares. It is a natural reaction to an event such as this. Let's go get some coffee," he said. "The clerk said he would be up all night." He put on his second-favorite moose jumper and pulled trousers over his thermals.

Anna was already dressed. Her bed didn't even look like she had slept in it. She stared at the screen of her phone.

"I keep looking at this cloud," she said. "It was evil, and we didn't even know it. How can you not recognize evil when you stare at it?"

"Evil and deadly aren't the same," Cato said.

"I know."

They walked out of their room and headed toward the office, where the promise of twenty-four-hour coffee resided. Like in most American motels, their room opened directly onto the parking lot. The lots were completely full, and the big American cars sat there quietly, waiting until they were relevant. It was late and no one was around. Both of them shivered in the cold night air. The sky above was free of clouds, and it was below freezing.

They both stopped and stared at the night sky. The moon was swollen, yet barely on the threshold of gibbous. The stars assembled around it, dancing and sparkling in a merry circle. The remaining sky was now clear of stars; they had departed their traditional homes and assembled in a bright ring around the moon. There they danced around it in a sort of obscene ritual.

There was something terrifying about the rich darkness of empty space, and yet it was preferable to the perverse star dance 'round the moon.

"Do you see what I see?" Anna asked.

"Something very bizarre is afoot," Cato said. "I don't know if there is any scientific explanation for it at all."

"Maybe we got dosed at dinner?" Anna suggested.

"Maybe." Cato said. "But it's not exactly a good thing when being slipped acid is the best-case scenario for your troubles."

With mutual, unspoken assent, they chose to forgo their coffee and return to their room. They locked the door and sat there in silence for the long, cold hours of the night. Cato tried very hard not to think about how the stars had looked like an enormous tentacle in the sky.

CHAPTER 7

"You can't go home, of course," Orson told her. "They'll be watching for you there."

"We haven't been back to our place since Monday," Arlo added. "I don't even know what a shower looks like anymore."

"I've got the dog," Maggie said. "We can't go to a motel."

"Don't you have any friends you can stay with?" Orson asked. There was something in his tone, a feigned casualness, a sly questioning, that she didn't like. But paranoia was really overwhelming her.

"I can drop in on my dad," she said. "He'd be delighted to see me twice in a week." Her tone was sarcastic by habit, but she realized that he actually would like to see her again. Her last visit had been so brief and clinical.

Her eyes were on the highway. Weekend traffic wasn't too bad—the number of day trippers from Portland decreased significantly along with the temperature. The earthquake and mysterious happenings at the coast were making people afraid, making them stay at home behind locked doors. She thought she saw the two men in the cab exchange a look. They had cleaned up with wet tissues as best they could, but both would carry bruises for the next few weeks.

"Word," Orson said casually. "But they may have staked out your parents. It still might—"

"Just who are 'they'? What do they want?"

"Wait until we're safe," Orson said.

"Orson," Arlo narrowed his eyes. "We came out here to tell her. Let's not wait any longer."

Orson looked at him for a long time and then sighed.

"Alright, here's what we know. There is a group of cultists. They are deranged killers. I mean, they are capable of anything. It's thought that they corrupted the mind of Charles Manson in the seventies."

"You're kidding."

"No. The cult was quite active. And then the eighties came, and they just kind of disappeared."

"Just like good music," Arlo put in.

"And those were the cultists back there?" Maggie asked. She glanced at the mirror. There was a motorcycle a little bit behind her truck. Were they being followed?

"Indeed," Orson said. "Maybe even the ones that stabbed you. But these are just the petty low-life cultists. The bosses and their crew all left town."

"We're not sure why," Arlo added.

"How are you sure of anything? How did you get involved in this?" Maggie asked. Now there were two motorcycles behind her. Her palms were getting sweaty. "And what was the deal with the video you showed me?"

"We were … we were regulars at Shoggoths. Even back in the day, when it was in the basement. Every once in a while someone would get drunk and say something strange," Arlo said. The motorcycles were definitely getting closer now.

"We began to put the picture together," Orson said. "No one else did because no one else knew there was anything to look for."

"If you knew there were cultists at the bar, why did you ask me to go there?"

"That was a mistake," Arlo said.

"We underestimated them," Orson admitted. "We thought we could show them to you. Some of them are no longer human. Get you to believe us. But we didn't know you'd get attacked."

"We were attacked, too," Arlo said. "Or else we could have helped you."

"You were attacked? How did you survive?" she asked.

"We are LARPers," Orson said.

"Live action role play," Arlo said. "We know all kinds of useful stuff."

"Including how to fight. Three years of tae kwon do for Arlo, and I am a master fencer, if I do say so myself," Orson said.

"Okay," she said dubiously. "But how did you know? What tipped you off?"

Both men were silent again. The motorcycles were right behind her now. Maggie felt like screaming, but she maintained her cool. Both bikes passed her; neither rider so much as glanced at her truck. They sped off ahead of her.

Her knuckles were white from gripping the steering wheel too hard.

"I think we're safe," Arlo said. He and Orson had followed her gaze, interpreted her fear. They had watched the motorcycles disappear into the distance with her.

"Unless they went to get more friends," Maggie said.

"I don't think so," Orson said, "Not their style. They have a leader, a person known as the Accursed. They whisper of him in fearful tones. I get the feeling that all decisions run through him. That said, the sooner we get off the 84 the better."

"We can take the scenic highway," Maggie said. "But it's slower."

"Speed is not our ally now," Orson said. "Secrecy is." Maggie wondered if he always talked like this, like he thought he was Aragorn from *Lord of the Rings*. The slightly amused, slightly annoyed look on Arlo's face suggested that he did.

"As to the video," Arlo said. "We don't really know. But you should know that the cultists are not really the threat here."

"No?" She turned off the highway at the first exit, headed for the old highway that had been built in the 30s by Roosevelt's CCC program. By modern standards, it was narrow and hard to navigate, but also incredibly beautiful—a corridor filled with mossy trees and tumbling waterfalls. "Sure felt like it to me."

"No," Orson said, taking over. "This sounds incredible. You may find it hard to believe."

"Let me guess," Maggie said. "You think Cthulhu is waking up, and that's why the plates are moving back together, why the compasses don't work, and why earthquakes and tsunamis are destroying the coast."

"On the other hand," Arlo said with a grin, "you may just already know."

"And these cultists want to wake him up?" Maggie asked. "And it's up to us to stop him?"

"Not exactly," Orson said. "Why do you say 'him'? Human gender isn't relevant to the Great Old Ones."

"One thing is as good as another, I guess," Maggie said.

"We're afraid that it's already been woken up," Arlo added.

"It's up to us to see if any humans can survive the awakening at all."

"So that was him in the video?" she asked. They weren't far from her father's place now, and she was beginning to relax. The tension in her stomach and lower back was slowly unwinding.

"No," Orson said. "We don't know what that was. Think lesser monsters, Godzilla types, trapped at the bottom of the sea with him for millennia."

"Maybe," Arlo added.

"Sure, we're not dealing in mathematical absolutes here," Orson said.

"So if Cthulhu rises, how can we fight him?" Maggie asked.

"That," Orson said, "is a very good question."

They reached her father's house on top of the hill a few minutes later. She was half-expecting it to be in flames, to be surrounded by motorcycle-riding maniacs, to be crawling with monsters from the sea.

Instead, it was empty. Her father wasn't even there. She let them in, and they made tea and switched on the news. Kamuks had a doghouse in the backyard, and she gave him some food and water. He whined at her. He was complaining, she thought, about the lack of a hike.

"Sorry, pooch," she said. "Maybe next time." It was a lie that even a dog could sniff out, and he didn't stop whining. She petted his head and then went to find Orson and Arlo in the house.

The TV was on. It was then that they saw that the Bridge of the Gods had fallen. It lay with one end on land and one in the river, like a discarded children's toy. The sight of the broken bridge was somehow shocking to Maggie. That bridge was part of her earliest memories. It had seemed as stable as anything in the world. And now it was broken, fractured as easily as she might snap a toothpick. It left her feeling unsettled.

Her dad arrived home about an hour after they had gotten settled. He stared at the two young men for a while but invited them to stay and introduced himself. Maggie told him everything she had learned. His face didn't change at all, not even as her story grew more and more outrageous.

At last she finished. Her father went and got a beer from the fridge, opened it, and then had a long sip.

"You don't drink," she said.

"I didn't," he said. "Not for almost twelve years now. But sounds like the world is ending. I reckon I had better start."

Maggie stared at him. "You believe me? I don't even believe me. How can you believe me? And why do you have a beer ready if you don't drink?"

Her father shrugged. His hair, long and gray, moved minutely with the gesture. "I like to be prepared, Magpie. Anyway, you don't take drugs. And you're not creative enough to make something like that up."

She laughed at that. His face creased in concern at the manic sound of it.

He put his beer down and wrapped his arms around her. "You're my little girl," he murmured. "I always knew you'd be special."

"Uh," Orson said. "Maggie? Leonard? You might want to see this."

On the news was a big man with slicked-back hair, a blue bandana, and a faded leather vest. A biker type, who was covered in nearly as many bruises as tattoos. He was standing in front of a burning building.

"Turn it up," Maggie said.

They listened as the man described the cult and the terrible things they would do. He seemed crazy, of course, but what he said made too much awful sense. At the bottom of the screen it said, "Wasp—ex-cultist."

"It's all going to hell now," Wasp said. "Kiss your loved ones because we don't have long left to live."

"Are you in danger?" the reporter asked.

"You bet your ass I am. They see this, the Brotherhood will kill me. But they already wanted to." He turned and stared straight into the camera. "You hear me? You should have killed me when you had the chance!"

The program quickly returned to the tanned skin and bleached teeth of the studio, and Maggie switched the screen off.

"You know what?" Orson said. "I think we should track down this dude."

Arlo nodded slowly. "Who better to fight cultists than an ex-cultist?"

"Are you two out of your minds? How could we trust him, even if we could find him?" Maggie asked.

"Well, these two boys found you, didn't they?" Leonard observed. There was a note of warning in his tone.

"Come to think of it, how did you find me?" she asked. "And call me?"

"We, uh, had an inside source," Arlo said. "Told us you were going hiking. So we drove out to Cascade Locks."

"Wait." Only a few people had been privy to her hiking plans. She knew her dad hadn't ratted her out. "Who told you about me?"

"Um, it was your coworker. Dave. We are old friends," Orson said hastily. "He worries about you."

"Dave? Excuse me? I trusted him!"

"Anyway," Leonard said, cutting in, "if there is a chance at keeping the world alive, I'd bet dollars to donuts that this Wasp character knows what it is."

"How do we find him?" Maggie asked again.

"Well, that's the question, isn't it?" Orson asked.

"I bet Dave knows," Arlo said.

"I wouldn't mind having a chat with Dave, either," Maggie said, her face rigid with anger.

CHAPTER 8

They spent the night at her father's. Maggie tried to call Dave several times, but there was no answer. That worried her. But he often went backpacking into the gorge, cowboy camping under the clouds, even in the winter. She had a bad feeling about it, though, and tired as she was, it was hard to sleep that night. Her dad had offered his bed, but the couch was fine, and Arlo and Orson didn't complain about the floor.

When she did fall asleep, long after slipping into her sleeping bag, her dreams were frightful nightmares.

Maggie is on a city bus, a friend sitting next to her. But he keeps pulling her breast out of her shirt. She slaps his hand away, but it is not her friend at all, she realizes. It is one of the attackers wearing a ski mask covered in tentacles. These are writhing, live things that stretch for her. She recoils in fear.

She is not on the bus anymore but downtown, next to the beaver statue. It is raining, cold rain, but as she looks up, she realizes it is raining fish. The tentacle man is gone, forgotten, and she runs for cover as cold clammy fish fall on her. They glow an evil, sickly green, and where they touch her skin, it burns and withers. The city itself is crumbling from the rain of sea creatures, moldering and decaying before her eyes. Buildings collapse with rumbling sighs, the Willamette River dries up almost instantly, and fuzzy green mold climbs over the ruins. In moments Portland is an ancient ruin.

Maggie sat up on the couch, her heart beating quickly and her forehead covered in sweat.

"I've got to stop dreaming about fish," she said. Outside, the sky was already light and she guessed it was after seven. Her injured hand ached. She got up and changed the bandages and then put some coffee on, careful not to wake Orson and Arlo, who were still sleeping on the floor.

She thought about cooking pancakes, but it seemed like too

much effort, so instead she cooked up a big batch of oatmeal. Her father joined her once the scent of coffee filled the house. His eyes were haunted and dark rings hung under them.

"Bad dreams?" she asked.

He nodded once with surprise. Arlo and Orson woke up similarly groggy. Breakfast was eaten in a wounded, wondering silence as everyone fought for control of their very minds, trying to wrest their thoughts from the clutches of the nightmares. Some extra-strong coffee helped. After breakfast they decided to go pick up Dave and then head into the city and try to pick up Wasp's trail. Maggie made the difficult decision to leave Kamuks at her dad's. She was coming back that night, after all, and it wasn't good for him to be tied up in the back of the truck all day.

They had been driving for a few minutes, all of them silent, when Maggie spoke.

"My dad is all the family I have. My mom left early. Tribal politics. But you two should find your families. Get them out of here. I'll give you a ride to Portland."

"Nah, we're with you," Arlo said slowly.

"We take this saving-the-world thing seriously," Orson said.

Maggie shook her head. These guys were hard to figure out. At times they seemed like clowns, but it seemed they were truly dedicated to this cause. Not that they weren't keeping obvious secrets from her. She noticed neither of them liked to answer questions directly. Maybe it was just that white boys in their twenties couldn't avoid a little innate buffoonery.

Dave lived in Hood River, which was a pleasant town of about eight thousand people and was famous for windsurfing and beer. Well, it was hard to find a town in this area not known for its beer, but one of the juggernauts of the craft brewing movement was here. And Dave lived up the hill from Full Sail Brewery.

Maggie parked outside his house. This early on a Sunday morning, not many people were about.

"This is his house, huh?" Orson said.

"I always thought it would be … I dunno, crazier," Arlo said.

"You've never been here? I thought you said you were friends," Maggie said.

"We are," Arlo affirmed. "We just usually hung out at

Shoggoths. Or our place. Once in a while, the Lovecraft."

As they spoke, they climbed up the stairs. The porch was empty, save for some empty Amazon boxes; Dave's front door was slightly ajar.

"Dave?" Maggie yelled into the house. There was no answer. She knocked loudly on the door.

"Dave's not here, man," Arlo said quietly. At Orson's look, he said, quite defensively, "Well, it had to be said."

"Come on in," a husky voice called from inside. The three people on the porch froze.

Arlo's eyes were really big.

"I don't think that's Dave," Orson said.

"It definitely isn't," Maggie said.

"Great. Let's get out of here," Arlo said. He walked back to her truck.

Orson hesitated, watching Maggie at the door and Arlo on the steps.

"Fuck it," Maggie said. She pushed the door open and stepped in.

"Word," Orson said.

Maggie didn't wait for either of them. She strode through the hallway. The kitchen, off to the right, was empty. The next room, the living room, was not. Maggie instantly recognized who sat there on Dave's sofa.

"You!" she said.

"And who," said the big man in the leather vest, "might you be?"

He had a gun in his hand, but he didn't even bother pointing it at her.

"I'm a friend of Dave's," she said. "Is he here?"

"I am afraid not," Wasp said. "Do I know you? You seemed to recognize me."

"We saw you on TV last night," a voice said from behind her. Orson and Arlo had joined her.

"You're the ex-cultist," Maggie said.

Wasp frowned. "Ex-member of the Brotherhood," he corrected. "I haven't lost faith in the Drowned One, but my leadership and experience are no longer wanted. Again." There was half a box of

Oreos next to him. Wasp grabbed three and put them in his mouth, chewing quickly. He ate three more and then drank from a container of milk to wash it down. Mouth empty again, he spoke. "Sit down. Wait with me."

"Is that a demand, or …" Maggie asked, with a look at his gun.

He laughed. "This little thing? No, I don't give a shit about you three. No offense. I'm just worried they might come after me. And I brought it in case he had any cats. Can't stand those evil, furry little fuckers."

"What?" Maggie asked.

"What do you want with Dave?" Arlo asked at the same time.

"Dave? That's what he calls himself? He hardly changed it at all. Cheeky. I'm not going to shoot him, if that's what you mean," Wasp said. "I just need to talk to him."

"Why? How do you even know him?" It seemed her mild-mannered coworker led a far more interesting life than she had guessed.

Wasp shrugged. "He was a cultist, too. Until I kicked him out. He's the only other ex-cultist I know."

Maggie sat down then, to hide her surprise.

Orson and Arlo joined her. The four of them sat there in the most uncomfortable silence ever. Wasp finished his package of Oreos, three at a time. Maggie couldn't stop staring at a small carpet on the floor. It had a round brown ring on it, like someone had set a cup of coffee on it. *Does Dave lie on the floor and drink coffee?* she wondered.

"So you were the Accursed?" Orson said.

"I was," Wasp said. "For a long time."

"What happened?" Arlo asked. He sounded genuinely curious.

"What happened is what always happens, hombre. Kids don't give a shit about the effort of those who came before them." He paused and then spoke again more quietly. "But maybe this was a top-up decision. Hell, maybe it was time I had to go. Maybe I shoulda stayed in Cusco," he said, before enigmatically adding, "My stone wasn't as strong as his."

Remembering what her father had said, Maggie asked, "Is there any way we can fight them?"

"Them? Maybe. Won't do you any good, though. You can't

stop He Who Sleeps. Not unless, well, you just can't." One of the tattoos on his arm, Maggie noticed, was a curved snake, eating its own tail. Didn't that have a name?

"There is a way, isn't there?" Orson asked. "You know something."

"Man, you don't get to come in here and question me." Wasp's eyes narrowed and his fingers gripped the butt of the gun more fiercely. *We should leave,* Maggie thought. *This man could kill us all.*

Instead, she said, "Do you want to get back at them or not? We can help you."

Wasp looked at the floor. He frowned heavily. "Ah, man, I don't know what I want." He stood up, so suddenly it shocked her. "You know what?" he said. His voice had the air of sudden, irrevocable decision. "Yeah, you can find more out. Not from me, though. Go out to the next meeting. Tomorrow night. It's a little place called Diamond."

"Diamond Lake?" Maggie asked. That actually wasn't too far away, just a few hours south down the 5.

He shook his head. His gray hair swung greasily as he did so. "Nah, too many people down there. This Diamond, it's in Harney County."

Maggie understood. "Oh," she said. "Oh. They're going out to Steens."

He nodded. "Indeed. Go carefully. Go quietly. If they catch you, the Brotherhood will kill you. But if you're serious about this, you may find out something of use. If you survive, and I'm still alive, and if we all survive our dreams, we can meet again."

He sat back down. No one spoke again for some time. Maggie felt a strange lassitude fill her skull. She looked at the rug on the floor again and didn't see any sign of a coffee stain. *What was going on?* Did Dave have anything to do with this?

Finally, she spoke without meaning to. "I can't believe Dave is a cultist. Was. He always seemed ..."

She trailed off, suddenly aware of what she was saying.

Wasp turned to look at her. She stared at his bruised, haggard, unshaven face, and it struck her again that she was sitting across from a very dangerous man.

"Seemed what?" he asked.

She shook her head.

"So level-headed? Like a reasonable human being? Such a good citizen?" he guessed.

"So intelligent," she said quietly.

Wasp grinned wryly at that, but he didn't say anything more.

Maggie felt emboldened. "Why do it?" she asked.

"Why?"

"Yes," she said. "Why destroy the world?"

"We're not stupid, you know," Wasp said. "Far from it. We are enlightened, a further step or two out of Plato's cave. The most important thing to understand—it's not our world. It's his. And he can do with it as he likes."

His words were uttered with the total conviction of a fanatic. "Even if that were true, and I don't know how you could know that, he's been asleep for millions of years. Don't we get squatter's rights?" Orson asked. He had been watching their conversation with great interest.

"If a flea crawls on you while you are sleeping, does that mean you have to let it stay?" Wasp asked.

"We're not fleas," Arlo said.

"And I still don't understand why you would choose to worship this thing," Maggie said.

"You don't understand," Wasp said. "Cthulhu is God, is the Buddha, is the Tao. He/It/She is the source of all human creativity, imagination, and endeavor. Only by tapping into his sleeping, pervasive consciousness did we ever climb out of the primordial ooze. We owe our very existence to his unsteady dreams. Indeed, we are only manifestations of his dreams. Why do you think there isn't life on any other planets? It all goes back to the Drowned One."

It was at that moment that Dave walked into the living room carrying a bag of groceries in his hand. He took one look at the four of them, dropped the bag to the floor, and turned and ran out the door.

CHAPTER 9

Although Oregon was known as a green and rainy place, new transplants were sometimes surprised to find that the state was actually two-thirds desert. Few people lived out here, and those that did were the descendants of the Oregon Trail pioneers, or those of a similar rural mind-set. It was a place nearly as empty as outer space, and Maggie like it that way.

In short, pretty much the entirety of eastern Oregon was a perfect place for a hidden cult meeting. But Maggie was more than up for the challenge. She reached the town of Diamond, which was merely a post office and a historic hotel clinging to the edge of nowhere.

She'd had a lot of time to think on the drive out. She'd come alone. Orson and Arlo would have come if she'd asked them, but they were afraid. She could see it in their eyes, when she dropped them off at their van. Likewise, although she wished she'd been able to bring her pooch with her, Kamuks was not a creature made for stealth.

Dave was gone. He had run out to his car and sped off down the hill. Wasp had hopped on his bike and followed him. Maybe the big biker meant him harm, she didn't know. She suspected she might not ever see her coworker again, regardless. There was too much she didn't know, and she longed for the simpler times of last week.

And yet here she was, out in the dry and cold. The ground was already covered in snow that was frozen solid and turning gray from dirt and pollution. It wasn't the kind of place she wanted to be, even not accounting for the murderous cult meeting. But she had never been one to shirk her duty.

She soon found traces of the cultists as she approached Steens Mountain. She could hardly read the wind, but following the tire tracks of dozens of cars was no real challenge at all. These cultists, dark and malevolent as they might be, were still born-and-raised city folk. They had parked their motorcycles and pickups in a sloppy heap at the end of an unpaved government road.

Maggie parked her truck off the trail. It was still late afternoon but already growing dark, and night fell quickly this time of year. She could smell smoke, could see hazy orange light, could hear the heavy pounding of drums. Rhythmic and driving, the drums reminded her of a ruffed grouse in the spring. The cultists certainly weren't trying to be quiet.

Maggie padded through the darkness as the sounds grew louder. She slipped around, approaching the gathering from deeper into the desert rather than from the highway. But there were no sentries; there was no sense of paranoia at all from these people. That seemed odd to her, she who had been living in fear since the night she had gone to Shoggoths. Then again, she wasn't protected by a gargantuan water god either. Maybe they had reason for their confidence.

On the ground was a pile of stones that had perhaps once marked some rancher's borders or family picnic spot. It went up about four feet, and Maggie dropped to her knees and peered over. Her injured hand throbbed from the pressure and she shifted slightly.

It was her first real look at the gathering; up until now she had been entirely focused on moving quietly and unseen. There were more people than she was expecting—two or three hundred. They were gathered around a bonfire, further proof they were not worried much about discovery. Maggie gasped. She was no prude, but this was gut-wrenching primal evil. Before her were cultists of all ages and all descriptions. She was horrified at what they were: many did not look human but looked like humanoid fish, bipedal frogs, octopus things, and creatures she could not readily describe. Some wore the same masks as those who had attacked her, she saw some carrying obsidian blades like the one that had cut her, and she wondered if any of them were her assailants. Some of the figures had no heads at all. Many wore robes and hoods, and even out here, in the snowy desert, she could smell the scent of the sea. The tallest of them all, inhumanly tall, had a face completely covered with barnacles and kelp. She could see its face in the firelight even beneath its dark hood.

Terrible as their forms were to behold, far worse were their actions. The cultists danced with each other, sticks of fire in their hands. As they danced, they stabbed each other with burning brands, cooking eyes and hands and ears of other dancers and then eating the cooked body parts while still attached . Maggie's stomach churned as she watched.

Not that the cultists seemed inclined to notice her. They continued their obscene, wanton rituals and wicked pleasures. Here, a limb was dancing. There, it was being chewed on while the owner of it gasped in pain and pleasure. Near the fire, two men penetrated a woman so close to the flames that her hair caught fire, and then her face. None of them stopped. The tall barnacle-faced being wandered through with aloof grace, like some obscene party host, and the frenzy continued. Though she saw no one add wood or fuel, the fire grew.

In the fire, she saw an indistinct image, a glimmer of something eldritch and wrong. A figure stepped out. It was the most bizarre thing Maggie had ever seen. She was staring at a thirty-foot-tall orca. It sounded ridiculous—it should have been laughable—but her heart started beating more quickly, and she felt sweaty, even in the cold. All the disgust and revulsion she had felt was gone, replaced by fear and unrelenting terror. She knew instinctively who this was. The cult's leader. The Accursed.

And then the giant was gone. It happened so quickly, and it was already so dark, that she wasn't sure what had happened. But there in the orca's place was a young, normal-looking man who she hadn't seen before. The cultists prostrated themselves before him, falling onto the ground like Tibetan Buddhists.

The barnacle-faced creature was the only one who didn't begin genuflecting. Maggie could see it gesticulating. The Accursed then turned and pointed away from the fire and the cultists and the revelry. He pointed, in fact, straight toward Maggie. Barnacle Face strode toward her immediately, covering the ground quickly. Maggie did not waste time wondering how they had found her, or if it was indeed her that they were looking for. She scrambled up and away and sprinted back toward her truck.

She didn't even look back, but she knew that the creature was catching up with her. She ran faster, feet barely touching the ground. Her truck wasn't so far away. She could maintain this speed for another minute or two. She was fast, but not nearly fast enough. A hard, clammy appendage grabbed her shoulder with enough force that she went tumbling to the ground.

She was up again in an instant, but a great rushing sound filled her ears, and the creature scooped her up in its arms. The tall skinny thing carried her bundled like a baby. It felt like falling, dream falling, where there is no context other than sensation itself, no time for fear or worry or awareness.

And then she was at the bonfire. None of the cultists even noticed her, but the Accursed watched her with interest. She could tell that he wasn't entirely human. The "whites" of his eyes were, in fact, a rich, dark black.

"Park Ranger got lost?" he asked.

"Not exactly," she admitted. She would have added more but couldn't think of a single plausible explanation.

He spoke again, this time not at her, but behind her. "There is no interest in this one. We will burn her with the Elder Sign and the Seal of N'gah," he said.

"No!" Maggie cried. "No!" But the Accursed turned away, his verdict rendered in stone.

"Tekeli-li," spoke the tall thing that held her. Its voice was as far from human as possible. A thousand faces stared at her in expectant joy.

Her fear, the urge to fight *and* to fly, flooded her as she recalled that struggle was possible. Her hands clutched at the chest of the thing carrying her in its arms. She pounded at its body with closed fists and flailed her legs, but the barnacle-faced sea creature held her too strongly. As she struggled, the sensation of falling overcame her again. It was like passing out, into a dream of falling, but she was conscious of the cold night air, of the gray clouds overhead, of the roaring of the fire and the smell of wood smoke.

The barnacle beast knelt slowly and grabbed something from the ground. Maggie could not see what but knew something cold and leathery was being held to her. Two things, in fact: one was long and poked her and the other seemed densely heavy.

The cultists surrounded them, genuflecting toward Barnacle Face and chanting: "*Ee-ya, Ee-ya, Ee-ya, Ee-ya, Ee-ya.*" The chanting was deep and dark, and the first syllable stretched out more with every iteration. Some were still killing as they chanted.

This is how I die, Maggie thought. The idea depressed her more than it frightened her; surely, she could have done more with her life. The thing held her up, over its head, and she could see the flames were not mere fire but living beings in other dimensions. The fire was a portal to another place or places, and though she had no doubt that her body would burn in that fire, she suddenly feared her spirit would land in one of those far-off hells. It was terrifying. Reality itself was unhinged, and merely by staring through the fire, she grew insane, gibbering mad, as her mind splintered from the vision of a thousand other worlds.

Grimly, she closed her eyes, fought against those images. She kicked and punched at her captor and screamed at the top of her lungs. But nothing Maggie did helped. The barnacle-faced creature was too strong. She was thrown with the sign, with the seal, into the fire, where she burned and died.

***

On the other side of another universe, a million million galaxies away, several realities removed from this instance of our world, a pair of observers discuss Maggie's immolation.

"But that didn't always happen that way, did it?" the first one said.

"Always? No. Reality fractured when HE awoke. All is possible. She was in possession of the Sign, though she knew it not," replied the second.

"What about another universe? One where she didn't die? That's more interesting, isn't it?"

"'Tis certainly better for us. We cannot get away with this more than just this once, of course," the second observer said.

"That's all it should take."

***

Maggie felt the cold leathery packages pressed against her. Her hands searched for something she could fight with and found the best possible weapon—a four-foot-long branch, three short sharp branches on one side and two on the other. She was no palaeoxylologist, and it was too dark to see, but it felt like petrified wood.

It was the item they called the Elder Sign, and it was from a time before time.

As the barnacle-faced thing held her aloft, she whipped the Elder Sign into its head. It cracked the skinny creature's skull, and black bubbles leaked from the fractured wound. The sea thing dropped her. Maggie landed on her feet, and beheld the astonished glares of several hundred bloody cultists.

The chanting stopped abruptly. Barnacle Thing had both hands around its head trying to stop the flow of bubbling black slime. In perhaps a trick of the light, it seemed that the black liquid was filled with starry eyes. The cultists oohed and sighed in great pleasure. The Accursed stormed up from the darkness. When he saw the dark liquid starlight spilling from the thing's head, he cried in alarm and horror. When he saw Maggie standing beside it, he swelled with rage. His size doubled and then tripled and then was beyond comprehension.

Here again was the giant orca she had seen from afar. Cool predator eyes stared at her from far up in the sky. It took one rumbling step and crushed four cultists. Its mouth was a slavering, crunchy hell.

Maggie brandished her only weapon. She held the Elder Sign out in front of her, a cross clutched against a vampire. She never knew if the ward would have worked; for, in that moment, the shadowy sky ink coalesced into a many-eyed beast. "*Tekeli-li!*" it roared with the voice of an elephant. It too was enormous, though perhaps only half the size of the orca. That didn't stop it from springing into the air, landing on the back of the orca. The orca sank from the unexpected weight and fell into the fire. It was big enough to put the fire out; the air smelled strongly of burnt rubber.

Maggie saw none of it; as soon as her captor was distracted, she turned and fled to her truck, clutching the Elder Sign tightly in her right fist. She drove back through the night, stopping only for gas and energy drinks.

Of the cultists, fewer than thirty would survive that night. Those that weren't crushed were eaten, and those that remained would face brutally cold temperatures with no fire. None of the survivors ever spoke of what transpired that night. As for the only other observers, across the galaxy, they were each quite pleased with the night's eventual happenings.

CHAPTER 10

Not long after Maggie climbed into her truck, in the cool hour of dawn, there were more giant waves at the Oregon coast. They slammed into the ruined, abandoned coastal towns. Many a coffee shop and seafood restaurant were reduced to flotsam and jetsam that night. Following the storm—indeed, creating the tsunami that carried itself—was an ancient being of vast size and still vaster powers. The long slumber was finally over, and he—it—was awake again. Awake and mobile, shaking off millions of years of sloth and seaweed.

Cthulhu had risen.

The towns were empty, but not unprepared. An elite force of veterans was assembled nearby, and there were three AC-130 gunships waiting to carry them. These men were veterans of Afghanistan, of Iraq and Mali and Somalia and Yemen. Former Green Berets and Delta Force and Rangers, these were men who entered battle with no name or rank. These men had long hair and beards, but they moved with the unmistakable swagger of trained killers.

The newest of them was a man named Billy Crow, and he, like the others, hadn't been told anything about what this was about. Other than it probably wasn't terrorists. And that it was maybe going to "get weird."

Billy Crow didn't mind weird. Hell, after some of the places he'd seen, he didn't know what weird was anymore. After what he'd seen in Peru, nothing could shock him. But he couldn't help but feel a little curious.

"You know anything about why we're here?" he asked the soldier sitting next to him.

The man only grunted.

Billy did not repeat the question. Instead, he sat and watched video feed of the US Army. There were probably fifty tanks heading to the Oregon coast, fifty tanks and a thousand soldiers. Regular soldiers, that is. Enough to handle anything short of full-scale invasion. His unit was on standby, just in case.

Someone across the room started shouting. Billy Crow followed the others to a large monitor. They could see satellite footage of something enormous crawling from the sea.

"Abashed the Devil stood, And felt how awful goodness is, and saw Virtue in her shape how lovely; saw, and pined His loss..." Billy muttered to himself.

It was hard to keep his eyes on the creature. It seemed to both be there and not exist at the same time. Like watching a 3D movie without the glasses. It seemed familiar. The face was reptilian, like that of a snake or lizard or dragon, with long kraken tentacles stretching around its mouth. But the body seemed almost like that of a man. A winged man, covered in meters-long red and green seaweed and other sea detritus, but humanoid in shape. It made his brain hurt and eyes ache to watch for too long.

But watch for too long is exactly what Billy Crow and a dozen other men did.

The creature rose, growing or stretching or unfurling, and it was big, big as a mountain. The few buildings that had not been crushed by the waves it utterly destroyed as it smashed its way inland. With powerful footsteps it crushed buildings to splinters and bricks.

The army tanks—Abrams and Wolverines and a few Dragonfires—arrived moments later. They were armored to withstand a major shelling. They were equipped with enough firepower to level a city. They were doomed.

The shots fired hit the ocean beast directly. Not a shell missed. The whoomping of the Dragonfire mortars was inaudible, but Crow could hear it in his mind. It was not a sound easily forgotten by those who had heard it even once.

The creature, whatever it was, should have been knocked back to the Jurassic. But it absorbed the weapons' fire. Possibly, it grew again, though not all watching would agree on what they saw.

Billy Crow suddenly knew what the monster was.

"That's Cthulhu," he said. "Elder God or Ancient One or something like that." He wasn't sure exactly what the difference was. But he was pretty sure it didn't really matter.

No one paid him much attention, which suited him just fine. He wasn't listening to any of their babble either. He stared at the screen, his eyes big as a child's on Christmas.

Cthulhu moved forward. With an enormous foot it stepped down and crushed two or three tanks. Crushed them flat and smashed them into the ground.

Many of the Special Forces, bitter and veteran though they were, gasped at that.

"There's no force on earth that can do that," someone said.

Tanks are supposed to be the things that crush other things, Billy thought.

They watched helplessly as Cthulhu destroyed the rest of the tanks. Some, he picked up and flung a few hundred meters into the sky. Others, he grabbed with long meaty tentacles and bashed them together. The Dragonfire mortars were swallowed whole.

In under a minute, there were no tanks remaining, merely jumbled piles of wrecked, smoking metal.

Billy was on the AC130 moments later. No one spoke. The confidence of the Joint Operation Special Forces was unshakable. But the soldiers on that transport were not happy. The sound of their rifles being loaded filled the air. As they drew closer, the silence grew more tense.

"How are we supposed to fight this thing?" a man they knew as Hawk asked. Hawk was a true warrior; he wasn't scared of anything, but right now that's exactly how he sounded.

"Not head on," said their commander, a man they all called Pigeon. All eyes turned to see him as he entered from the cockpit. Pigeon was tan and had a scruffy brown beard. "Head on is not our strength. I do not want you to engage. Watch, learn, and live. We'll determine a weak point, and we'll hit it hard."

Billy sniffed and gagged. It smelled like a thousand open graves on a hot summer day.

"Hell!" he shouted the same moment a massive dragon claw plucked their plane from the sky. It had been flying low, but not so low that a creature standing on the ground should have been able to grab it.

Their trajectory changed as they went hurtling toward the ground as Cthulhu flung them away with colossal force.

The plane hit the ground, and all was chaos. Some few men, hardier or luckier than the rest, scrambled out of the wreckage.

Their guns were ready, but what they saw there, they never spoke of again. They never spoke of anything again. One direct look at the moving mountain that had climbed from the sea scrambled their brains. Their connection with reality was severed, instantly and irrevocably.

Crow could not move. His arm was pinched in collapsed metal from the side of the plane, and he was losing too much blood. Many of the soldiers on the plane were dead from impact. Pigeon lay next to him with his head smashed in and blood leaking out, dripping on Crow. The ground shook with heavy footsteps, and Crow cried out each time as the metal pinched his arm deeper and tighter.

There was only one course of action. He grabbed his knife. Before he could start to saw at the bone, the plane shifted. His arm popped up, but it was with so much pain that he passed out.

***

Something shook him awake a few moments later. It was no longer dark but the cloudy relative brightness of day. Crow realized he had been out for hours, not minutes.

Hawk shook him again. "You still alive?" he asked.

"Yeah, man, I'm still here."

"Who are you?" Hawk asked.

Billy stared at him, not understanding the question.

"What's your name?" Hawk asked again.

And then Billy saw his eyes.

"Your eyes!" he said. "You're blind."

Hawk frowned. "Shrapnel in my eyes when we landed. Need to get it fixed up. 'Til help arrives, I think it's just you and me."

"Everyone else is dead?"

"Dead or worse. Everyone who saw that thing went crazy. Ran off onto the highway shooting their guns. Whatever world they see, it ain't this one."

"*Freely they stood who stood, and fell who fell,*" Billy said, mostly to himself. "And Cthulhu?"

"Is that what you call it?"

"Yeah, that's what I call it," Crow said.

"Well, Cthulhu headed inland, near as I can tell. Heading toward Portland."

"How long do we have?" Billy asked. "Until it makes it?"

Hawk shrugged. "I have no idea."

"Guess?" Billy asked.

"Well, from what I can hear, he doesn't seem to be rushing. If that's what you mean. This world is new to him, right? The army will keep attacking him, and that will slow him down just a little. I'd guess we have two, maybe three, days until Cthulhu reaches Portland."

CHAPTER 11

On their Harleys, with their guns, bodies wrapped in black leather, they came at dawn.

Cato and Anna had not slept, could not face the terrors of their dreams. All night they had tried to come to grips with the dystopian reality that now seized them. Thus, when the rumbling of engines and the firing of guns sounded from outside their room, it seemed like the natural culmination of events, like the step they had been waiting for without realizing it, rather than a sudden catastrophe.

They slipped quietly out of their room with little other than their clothes and Anna's phone. Anna wished she had packed better, but yesterday had been a day trip to the beach. *Was it only yesterday? Could the world change so much in twenty-four hours?* Perhaps that was how everyone felt when confronted by tragedy— a world brimming full with infinite private apocalypses.

There were more bikers than she could easily count in the dark morning sky. The lights of their bikes shone like beacons from the center of the parking lot, and they laughed coarsely. All carried weapons, rifles and pistols and baseball bats. They wore ski masks with tentacles dangling from them. The bikers had caught the young Pakistani clerk who worked the front desk and had staked him out in the parking lot. Anna was not sure what kind of torture they were performing, but the man was screaming and pleading with them to stop.

Their room was on the corner, and she and Cato eased around the edge. They paused there, out of sight of the bikers.

"They are torturing him," Cato said.

"I know," Anna said.

"Can we save him?" he asked.

"No. How could we?" Anna said.

"It's not right," he said.

"Cato. Come on," she said. She knew it was sad, but she felt nothing but relief. Better him than them. At this point, the two of them could only choose to join him in torture and suffering. Which perhaps they yet would, but she wanted to make that as difficult as possible.

The highway ran next to the motel, separating it from a large forest of firs. She pointed to the trees, and Cato nodded as gunshots fired behind them. His breath steamed in the cold air as he exhaled slowly. There were no cars on the road. Everyone who could flee had fled.

"Who are they?" Cato asked.

"Bike gangs, end-of-the-world militias, Mad Max wannabes, something like that," Anna said. *The kind of people who buy the guns we make*, she thought but did not say. Guilt was a corrosive luxury they could not currently afford.

"Their balaclavas had tentacles," Cato said. "It made me think of Lovecraft. I knew something impeccably bleak was coming. The stars told me."

The fact that this didn't sound at all crazy should have worried Anna.

"It won't stop with the clerk. They'll kill everyone at the motel," Cato said.

"What can we do? They have rifles. I was lucky to charge my phone last night," she answered.

"You're right. Let's stay close to the road. Try to warn someone about this. Maybe they can call the police."

She nodded. "My phone isn't working. 911 is down. And there is no wi-fi. But I'll keep checking."

"Right. Let's go."

Shoulders hunched, heads down, they stalked across the cold pavement. At the renewed sound of gunfire, Anna could not resist a look back at the parking lot. The clerk lay still and silent as the bikers shot into motel rooms and captured the people who ran terrified from their rooms.

One brown-masked biker glanced up and saw the two Norwegians, halfway across the road. He shouted something, waving his gun in the air, and three bikers joined him. They sprinted toward the pair.

"*Faen*," Anna swore. The two of them rushed into the woods. This close to the highway, the trees were not dense, and it was not as easy to disappear into them as she had hoped. Low lying, woody bushes clung to their legs and stabbed at them, making it impossible to go quickly.

A gunshot sounded from way too close, and the spindly pine tree to her right splintered.

Cato growled in anger and pulled her away to the left. Three more shots rang out but none hit them. The scientists ran now, their legs shattering the woody bushes on the ground. Anna was tired and afraid and utterly unsure of her place in the world, but she was also fit and full of adrenaline. She could run forever. They pushed on.

The trees around them grew denser. They slipped into a copse of trees and pushed through it. *Stop.* They could run no more, and now silence mattered as much as speed. The trees around them now were massive, some as high as a six-story building The ground was littered with fallen branches and enormous pinecones. It was hard to maneuver, but together they slithered through the wood until they came to the brink of a large cliff.

A ravine stretched before them. It was covered in scree and too steep and rocky to glissade down. And it stretched on either side of them as long as they could see.

"Ah, hell," Cato said.

"We go down," Anna said.

"We will break our legs. If we're lucky."

"Maybe," she said. And then she jumped down the cliff. She slid for ten meters or so and caught herself on a tree. Large boulders dotted the area around her.

"Come on," she shouted up to Cato. He had a slight fear of heights but usually overcame it without hesitation.

Cato looked back, and Anna heard a gunshot. Cato leaped down and slid down the scree slope until he was close to Anna.

Anna pulled him behind the boulder to her right. "Stay here," she said. Peeking over the edge of the rock, she saw six cultists, all in tentacle ski masks, hovering around the edge of the precipice. *More of them? Like they needed reinforcements*, she thought. *Cowards.* None of them wanted to slide down the precipice, not when there were easier targets back at the hotel. They'd come to shoot fish in a barrel, not descend down a ravine to hunt unknown enemies.

Or so she hoped. Anna ducked back down to make sure they

didn't catch sight of her. "Let me see your arm," she whispered. Cato frowned in concentration. She held it carefully in her hands and peeled back his sweater. He had been lucky. The bullet had grazed his arm but had not pierced him. It would hurt, and he would bleed, but the wound was fine. She told him that, although with his military background he already knew it. It was nice to hear good news from someone else, sometimes.

Cato sighed in relief.

"But, it's not all good news. You've got blood on your grandma's jumper," she said.

"Damn. That's the worst thing to happen so far," he said.

Anna peeked out from the rocks again. There was no sign of the biker gang. She doubted they were stealthy enough to creep down the scree slope unnoticed, but it was still time to go. The longer they stayed in one place, the more vulnerable they would be. And without movement, their bodies would cool and they risked hypothermia.

They made their way down the slope, going on their bums at times. When it leveled out, they walked eastward, or as close to it as they could guess. The silence around them grew and filled the forest with fear. Anna could feel eyes on her from all directions, but every time she looked, there was nobody there. Cold miserable droplets of rain fell.

By mutual decision, after a few hours of pushing their way through bushes and over boulders, they hiked back up the cliff wall and headed toward the road. Thick fir trees surrounded them. "Ah," Cato said. He smiled as he rubbed the thick trunk. "*Pseudotsuga menziesii*. The evergreen conifer."

"Pine or fir?" Anna asked.

Well, it's a Douglas fir. But it's not really a fir."

Both were lost in their own thoughts, and the need for silence remained. The slope had leveled out, and they reached the side of the highway without breaking a sweat. There were no cars on the road, no birdsong in the forest. Anna checked Cato's wound again, but it was barely bleeding.

"I know the reason we came to America wasn't exactly humanitarian," Cato said.

"Desalination will help everyone," Anna replied.

"The real reason," Cato said.

"I know," she said. "The R99."

"Yeah. There will be blood on our hands. But that doesn't bother me. We're just humans, violent monkeys. But leaving those people to die …"

"There's nothing we could have done," she said wearily.

"There might have been," he said. "If we'd had it with us."

"We couldn't have known," she said. "It was a day at the beach."

"We need to survive long enough to get back to Portland. We can defend ourselves there," Cato said.

"And then we can avenge those people," Anna said.

"Shhh," Cato said. "Do you hear that?"

In the not-so-far distance, they could hear motorcycles engines. And they were coming closer.

CHAPTER 12

Her feet brush the sand. With her big toe she sketches a line in it. She adds two strokes on one side and three on the other. The image in the sand glows. It is captivating. Maggie stares at it with excessive interest.

At last the wind blows too hard and too cold for her to ignore. She shivers, can't stop shivering. She pulls her jacket around her and looks up. Around her the gray sea looms like a hungry predator. The gray clouds and the gray water merge, and there is no horizon, no there, *only her, only here.*

But the sea, she realizes, is not gray at all. It's black, murky and somber as the darkest night. And, as dispassionate as it is deadly, it watches her. She glances down, but the sign in the sand is a mere collection of driftwood. Already the cold waves surge around her feet, pulling the wood into the foam's cold embrace.

She knows that losing the wood is a tragedy. But when she bends down to pick up the pieces, she starts falling and falling and falling. Around her are a thousand eyes filling the darkness. And though there is no mouth, they speak: "MAGGIE. US TO BACK COME."

She awoke, wrapped in a sleeping bag on her father's couch, to the smell of coffee. It was already ten in the morning, and in the light of morning her dream faded. The events of the previous night lay buried in her mind, readily accessible but not quite something she was ready to dredge through. It had all happened, though, of that she had no doubt. The Elder Sign, four feet of petrified wood, was propped up on the side of the couch. Her hand still ached, and her bandage was dusty and crusty.

Maggie looked into the kitchen. Leonard stood there, bent over the toaster. She could hear the knife scraping margarine over the crusty bread, could smell the toasted wheat and coffee in the air. When he saw that she was awake, he grunted and brought her a mug. There was something different about him that morning. He was wearing a collared shirt and a tie, and his long gray hair was combed and parted down the middle.

"How's Kamuks?" she asked.

"He's fine. Still sleeping out in his doghouse," he said. "You got in late last night."

She nodded, rubbing sleep from her eyes. "Why are you dressed up?"

"You alright, Magpie?"

"I'm fine," she said. "Why are you dressed up, Dad?"

"I guess you already know that."

"You're going to see them, aren't you?"

"That's about the size of it," Leonard said, sipping from his own coffee. He always drank it with a bit of creamer.

"Why?" Maggie sat up. The sleeping bag fell down to her knees. "You know what they will say. The same crap they say every time."

"I have to try," he said.

"It's politics!" she said. "You can't fight politics. Their lawyers won't let any of their precious money slip through."

He hesitated. "Well, it's never a good time. But I have to try now."

"Why now? She didn't come back?"

"Your mom? No."

Maggie sighed. Her mom had never recovered from her ten years in prison in the late eighties. She'd been caught by police for selling marijuana, and that had been at the height of Nancy Reagan's "Just Say No" America. That her mom had been trying to make money for Maggie's books and school fees was a guilt that had grown as she had aged. But resentment lived inside her, too—she had seen her mom only three or four times since she'd gotten out.

"I wanted to talk to you about those friends of yours," Leonard said. "I know you're an adult. You can make your own decisions. But—"

"But, you don't want me seeing them again?" Maggie asked.

He shrugged. "I didn't say that. But how well do you know them? Can you trust them?"

"Are we doing this again?"

"It's my job as your parent," he said. "I didn't want to say anything in front of them. I know you hate it when I embarrass you. But I have to look out for you. I've been doing it since the eighties. It's not just something I can turn off, you know."

"What do you suggest?" Maggie said.

"Get off the grid. Go deep into the woods. Never come back." He said it with no hesitation at all. Maggie realized he had been thinking about this for some time.

"That's just running away," she said. "If we can fight this, we need to."

"Some battles can't be won," her father said.

"Some battles are won simply by fighting them," she answered, her voice raising a little.

At that moment, the phone rang. Her father answered and handed it over to her. It was Orson.

"How did it go last night?" he asked.

She wasn't sure how to describe it, so she went with the safest option. "It was strange."

"That doesn't surprise me," he said. "There is some seriously weird shit going on at the coast."

"Creatures coming out of the sea?" she asked.

"You could say that. I fear the worst—Cthulhu has returned to the mortal realm."

"That's not all," Maggie said. "There are other monsters, too. I saw one last night."

"Word," Orson said. "Hey, we're almost there. Be ready in twenty minutes. I have something to show you."

She hung up. Her dad looked concerned but said nothing. Maggie sipped at her coffee and went out to greet her dog. He looked at her very seriously, as though appraising her.

"Weird dog," she said.

When she came in, a little wet from the morning rain and her hands infused with the scent of wet dog, her father had turned on the news.

"You gotta see this," he said in a voice brimming with quiet horror.

Maggie stared at the television.. Towns had been ripped from the earth, leaving only the gaping holes of their foundations. Fires burnt through old growth forests, and long dormant volcanoes were spewing smoke into the sky again. There was grainy drone footage of US soldiers fighting some kind of moving mountain. When she realized what the mountain was, Maggie had to sit down and catch her breath.

A few minutes later, a forest green 1984 Vanagon pulled up into her father's driveway. Maggie recognized it from the parking lot at Cascade Locks. Orson and Arlo stepped out. Each had a long sword strapped to his waist. It was drizzling lightly, and Maggie was wearing a bright blue rain jacket. Orson wore a long trench coat, and Arlo looked somehow comfortable in his t-shirt.

Orson twirled in his trench coat.

"Who do I remind you of?" he asked. "Connor MacLeod, right?"

"I don't know who that is," Maggie said.

"Another time," Arlo said, forestalling Orson's impassioned explanation.

"Those are real swords. Where did you get them?" she asked, pointing to their weaponry.

"One of our LARPing friends is a smith and leather maker," Arlo explained.

"These blades are as sharp as anything," Orson said. "And the balance is perfect."

Maggie thought about what she had seen at the cult meeting the night before. "Did you see the news? They said that an entire army battalion was destroyed this morning. I don't even know how many people are in a battalion."

"I'm not sure, either. Maybe around five hundred," Orson said.

"I thought more like a thousand," Arlo said.

"It just keeps getting worse," Maggie said. After a few moments of standing in the rain, she said, "I'm not sure how much those swords are going to help."

"They'll be as much use as that cane you are carrying," Orson said. She hefted the Elder Sign into better view and examined it. The wood was dark gray, petrified and hard as stone. But there were slivers of an almost nuclear green running through it. Or so it sometimes seemed when she looked at it from the side.

Orson saw it, too, and he fell to his knees in shock. His mouth was agape; he didn't even seem to care that his knees sat in a small puddle.

"Is that what I think it is?" he asked in a voice barely above a whisper.

Arlo's eyes bugged out, too. "Where the blazes did you get that? And why didn't you tell us?"

"It's a long story," Maggie said. "But I think it saved my life last night."

"You've got the Elder Sign! I didn't even know if it was real," Orson rose and came to her, eyes filled with wonder. "You must have had some night."

"This changes everything," Arlo said. He was beside his friend, eyes equally big.

"Indeed. We must venture forth, to the coast," Orson said. Maggie noticed he was speaking like a fantasy character again and took that as a good sign. Then she really listened to what he was saying.

"Excuse me?"

"Maggie, we need to," Orson said. For the first time, his eyes left the Elder Sign and found hers. "We can stop Cthulhu. With that, we can stop it."

"It's maybe the only thing that can," Arlo said.

"This?" Maggie asked. She thought of the creature's skull splitting when she had hit it, and the unformed dark matter that had spilled out. "How?"

"Well, all this was myth," Orson said. "Until a few days ago."

"Some have speculated it's because the Elder Sign is made of nearly all right angles, the shape of which traps the non-Euclidean Cthulhu into our realm, where he can be defeated," Arlo said.

"I forgot about that theory," Orson said. "Another speculation is that the Sign contains the power of the Elder Gods. The primary opponents of the Great Old Ones, which Cthulhu belongs to. By owning it, you are claiming some of the power, some of the gravitas, of the Elder Gods. You are no longer just a human but a walker on the plane of Cthulhu himself. You are declaring: Cthulhu, I am your equal."

"Yeah, that is a good one, too," Arlo said. "And just being in its presence will keep you from going instantly insane."

"Insane?" she asked. "What do you mean?"

"That which man was not meant to know," Orson said. She realized he had something green stuck in his teeth. "Apparently the mere sight of Cthulhu pulverizes puny human brains."

Maggie felt completely overwhelmed. She thought of the argument with her dad and was tired of it all. The same argument, just dressed in different clothes. Maggie turned to Orson. "The coast, eh? You got room in your van for my pooch?"

CHAPTER 13

It was definitely a walking fish person. In his head, that sounded kind of cute, like something from Dr. Seuss. But this creature was not from any children's story. This thing was not cute.

Billy Crow tapped Hawk on the shoulder, their signal for him to stay low, stay quiet. *What are those things?*

The fish men shambled through the fields. They were tall, some almost seven feet tall. Their skins were green and gray, mottled with pink and ochre and black. They all sagged in the middle, round bellies protruding. Their faces were stretched long but pinched, and they smelled like rotting seaweed and brine. But the worst thing was their hands. Completely out of proportion with their bodies, their hands were incredibly wide, with flaps of skin connecting their fingers.

They moved through the field with a sense of purpose. Billy Crow recognized a predator when he saw one. There was no question that they would kill him as soon as they saw him. He wondered how humans tasted to fish. *Probably a little like chicken.*

One of the fish people cocked its head and ambled without urgency toward the two soldiers. It hissed, and the others turned and stared; then, they began to move toward them.

Billy sighed.

His MK14 was in his hand, and he aimed carefully at the first creature.

BLAM.

The headless body fell twitching to the ground. Yellow ichor spilled from the wound, steaming on the cold, hard ground.

The remaining fish men hissed collectively. Their speed increased significantly.

BLAM BLAM BLAM BLAM BLAM.

In under thirty seconds, they were all dead. Killing these things wasn't hard, and he had plenty of ammo, but the sound always drew more of them. And with a blind man in tow, Billy was neither as fast nor as stealthy as he wished.

"Come on," he said to Hawk. He helped the big man up, and they moved eastward. It was not raining today, and in fact there was more blue sky than clouds—what was referred to in this part of the world as a "sun break." They headed east, hoping to find some sign of civilization, if not reinforcements. The Pentagon was sure to have some contingency plan.

Crow was growing tired, though. They had been on the run without sleep for almost thirty hours now. At first, he had been surviving long enough for the next wave of Special Forces to come in, but it now seemed there were no more waves coming. Fish men filled the forests and the fields, and armed men on motorcycles ruled the roads. It was the worst place Crow had ever been. The only good thing was that they had avoided running into Cthulhu again.

The worst had been yesterday just before dusk when they had found Jay. His eyes were unfocused, and he had been chatting to himself. The words he said made no sense. When he sensed them, he screamed and pissed himself. Then he aimed his gun and fired. Billy Crow and Hawk would undoubtedly have died right there, save that Jay's rifle was long since out of ammo. They'd left him there, but later Billy thought it might have been kinder to eliminate his pain.

None of their electronic equipment was working, and the earth rumbled with distant earthquakes. So far, Crow was busy with the task of sheer survival, but in the back of his head, he lamented the lack of a plan. Billy Crow always had a plan. It was what had kept him alive in hot zones around the world.

"Hey, Billy," Hawk said.

"Yeah?"

"We're going to make it."

"I know, man."

"I know you do. But I'm telling you again. We're going to make it."

"Yeah. I know," Billy said.

"That was good shooting back there. I was counting your shots. And bodies hitting the ground. You didn't miss."

"Shut the fuck up," Billy said. "You did not hear the bodies hit the ground."

"It's true what they say, man. I feel my other senses getting better and better."

Billy smiled. "Okay, you ain't wrong. I didn't miss any. You're lucky you can't see those freaky things, though. I'm never eating sushi again."

"Not me. I'm going to eat nothing but fish sticks for a year. Teach those fuckers who's at the top of the food chain."

Billy laughed. "*Who overcomes by force, hath overcome but half his foe,*" he said.

"You quoting Shakespeare again?" Hawk asked.

"It's not fucking Shakespeare," Billy Crow said.

After they had been walking for a few minutes, Hawk said: "Tell me what you see."

Billy described the area as they walked through marshy wetlands. He pointed out the cracked earth and fallen trees. He noted the posts of old fences and the complete lack of animals. Hawk didn't say a thing, just listened and concentrated on keeping up.

At last, Crow felt they had come far enough from the gunshots. He paused to scout out the surrounding area. More fields and forests. It was either too open or far too dense for quick mobility. He looked behind him. From the coast came clouds like he had never seen before. They were sickly green, vibrant with unhealthy radiant energy. The clouds pulsated as they filled the sky.

"Oh, hell," Billy said.

"What?" Hawk asked.

"There are some fucked-up clouds overhead."

"Clouds? Don't do that, man. I thought we were really in trouble for a minute."

"Well, you can't see these clouds," Billy said. "They look nuclear. I'm afraid we maybe nuked that big monster."

Hawk whistled. "Never liked those Fallout games."

No rain yet fell, but the air was suffused with the reek of rotting meat and brine. Hawk sniffed the air with distaste clear on his face.

"What the fuck? Is it raining dead things?" he asked.

"Never seen anything like it," Billy said.

The ground rumbled. This time the earthquake was really close. Billy had to scramble to stay on his feet. The shaking came again, a few moments later, and again after that.

Billy Crow looked up, and now knew that it was no earthquake.

Above the tree line, from the sea, a massive beast strode toward them. It was starkly black and fiercely white, and it was taller than the tallest trees. The sound of cracking timbers filled the air as it snapped old growth trees with its enormous feet. It looked to Billy like water was flowing through the trees beneath the monster, and then he realized it was the rippling of hundreds of fish people marching with the thing.

At that moment, he saw the gargantuan thing more closely. Billy stared at it, aghast, and wished he could ask Hawk for a second opinion. But there was no question about it. It was a giant fucking killer whale.

"Hey, man, what's going on?" Hawk asked.

"You wouldn't believe me if I told you," Billy said.

"Is it *him*?" Hawk did not even try to hide the fear in his voice.

"I don't think so. This is a giant animal. But smaller than *him*."

"Animal? Anything specific?"

"I mean, it's kind of a giant fucking killer whale. But it's walking. It has arms and legs."

Hawk whistled. "Apex predator of the sea. They use pictures of those things to scare great whites away in South Africa."

"This one is really big."

"Are we fucked?" Hawk asked.

"No. Maybe. Yeah. We'll see," he said. "I'm going to see if I can slow it down."

He didn't hesitate. His MK14 was old but accurate as fuck and could hit a target eight hundred meters away. He raised it carefully to his eye. The great beast was well within range, and Billy could see the yellow of the orca eye gleaming through his iron sights. There were angry welts and blackened bubbling patches on the killer whale's shoulders and snout. Had someone tried to light it on fire? It was a risk, drawing the attention of the mob. But the chance to take out this giant was too good to dismiss.

It was an easy shot, and he nailed it. The giant orca bellowed, and the army of fish creatures lumbered toward Billy and Hawk.

The MK14 was the wrong weapon for crowd control.

Billy aimed again and fired three more times at the orca—once more at the yellow target that was its eye and twice at the left side of its chest, where its heart presumably was. The orca did not seem affected at all, and the mob of fish men drew closer.

"I'm guessing you didn't slow it down," Hawk said.

"Good guess. We gotta scoot."

He helped Hawk up, and they sprinted away. The blind man ran recklessly along a deer trail, and Billy ran behind him, shouting out directions and when to jump a pile of rocks or duck beneath low-hanging branches. They had never served together, but both had undergone vigorous training. They had also practiced combat blindfolded many times, of course, and had fought under pitch black moonless skies. But the knowledge that darkness was all that awaited him forever must be terrible to Hawk. Then again, forever might not be very long.

Billy turned and spied three fish men behind them. He yelled at Hawk to stop and fired at the trio of sea creatures. Two pitched to the ground, but one still came at him. It was pure monstrosity, its entire face a wide mouth full of pointed teeth. A little ball of light hung from its head. Billy fired again, hitting it in the stomach and the right leg just under the knee and through the mouth again. The fish man slowed but did not stop.

With booming steps, the orca lumbered closer. A single step covered ten or fifteen feet of pasture easily. It was now so close that Billy could hear its great heart beating.

"We are outgunned," Billy Crow said. "Take evasive action."

Hawk turned and jogged off, his hands extended in front of him.

Billy followed him, but something sharp caught his shoulder. He turned instinctively and punched, catching the sharp-toothed fish thing in the chest. It took a step back, but it was dense and heavy. It darted forward, mouth snapping, and Billy leaped back. He landed on his back, air driven from his lungs but rifle still in his hands. The fish man loomed above him, and he shot it twice. The bullets tore through its body, and it slumped.

The orca and army of fish men were right behind it.

Billy rose and fled without another backwards look. He had not gone far when he found what was left of Hawk.

The man's body lay on the ground, and kneeling over it, tearing at his flesh like wolves, were half a dozen more sharp-toothed fish men. They reminded Billy of piranhas. He fired blindly at them as he ran. One fell, maybe, while three rose to chase him.

Billy ran east, away from the army of fish-headed monsters. He zigged and zagged into a forest too large and dense for the giant orca to follow. He ran for fifteen minutes, until he reached a very steep cliff. He caught himself by grabbing onto a dead, leafless tree, and the branch broke off in his hand. Below him, several hundred meters below him, was the Columbia River. Billy closed his eyes as quickly as he could. For, in the river, and on the land around the river—so big was it that it waded both over land and through water at the same time—was the mightiest of all beings.

Cthulhu.

Behind him, Billy Crow could hear a horrifying blubbing as the fish men closed in. Billy slid down the cliff and jabbed the branch into his eyes.

CHAPTER 14

Wasp couldn't find him anywhere. His old connections amounted to nothing. Everyone he had known in the halcyon days was dead or in jail or working at New Seasons. *Shoulda stayed down there in Peru*, he thought, *drinking pisco sours and worried about nothing so much as which happy hour to visit*. It was a nice thought. It would have only delayed the inevitable, though.

Wasp knew he was already a dead man. Most of the world, maybe everyone now living, would be dead soon. This did not trouble him. Mortality was not a fear of his. Humanity had had a good run, but all runs end. Being back in Portland brought back a lot of memories.

He hadn't left the group in the eighties of his own free will. Sure, the apparent failure of St. Helens had hurt his cred. And that maniac guru out in Antelope had siphoned away too many of his own followers. But Wasp had vision, and he could have turned it around. He'd had a lead on where to find the Elder Sign, and it was under his supervision that the Seal of N'gah had been obtained at great cost from the temple of Ulthar. There had yet been hope for the Brotherhood of the Sleeper, the Cult of the Cosmic Dream.

But one man had made it his mission to take him down: sowing dissent, casting aspersions, raising doubts; before long Wasp was unwanted by a large majority of his followers. Wasp had left in the middle of the night, with nothing more than a vague vision of Mexico in mind. He later learned the man who had ousted him had not even taken over as leader. Had causing Wasp's ruin just been out of some perverse sense of humor? That man, the man who had ruined him, now called himself Dave.

Wasp wanted to find his one-time comrade and have a serious talk. But "Dave" had years of experience living in hiding. He hadn't even left Portland after leaving the cult, yet the old fox had not been discovered.

And so, his quarry unavailable, Wasp sat in the Lovecraft Bar and drank PBRs and teenage zombies from an inattentive bartender. He had no idea what the latter was, but it was part of the unhappy hour special, and the rum they used was excellent. It reminded him of Flor de Caña, that Nicaraguan rum that was less a beverage and more a lifestyle.

He sat sullenly, alone. It was early enough that there were no crowds, no DJs, no dance floor. The way he liked it. The entire city, in fact, was starting to feel only half full. People were not showing up to work, failing to pick up their children from school. He ordered nachos and scraped the cheese off with his teeth. The soggy, empty chips he cast back onto his plate, their cheese delivery mission complete.

Wasp stared out the window, mulling his next move. It was hard, this being mortal again. His rock still sat in his pocket. It had splintered when his mighty opponent had beat him down, the town in flames, and Wasp had barely escaped with his life. The rock of R'lyeh had since been utterly inert. He did not dare try it again, not until things were considerably more desperate.

Another beer down and—lo!—he saw Dave walk by. Wasp hurled two twenties on the bar and burst out of the dark bar onto the street.

Dave turned at the sudden movement. When he saw Wasp, his face fell.

"You," Dave said. He swallowed his shock, restored a neutral expression. "You look old."

"You don't," Wasp said. "What dark god provided you with eternal youth?"

"Eh," Dave said, "I might look young. But I'm still ugly."

Wasp laughed. "Join me for a drink?"

Dave glanced around him. There were few people on the streets, though the adjoining street was a major thoroughfare and normally filled with traffic. It was an industrial area of town, and the buildings were all large and concrete.

"Don't suppose I got much choice," Dave said.

"Don't suppose you do."

Wasp opened the door for him, and they returned to Wasp's spot at the Lovecraft Bar. The lone bartender was still on her phone and had not even seen the cash on the bar. Wasp grabbed it and ordered more drinks.

After the first long swallow, Dave turned to him. He looked how Wasp remembered him, except his brown hair was long, past his shoulders, and there were worry lines etched on his face.

"So, what's on your mind?" Dave asked.

Wasp sighed. "End of times, man. Makes you think."

"We actually did it," Dave said. "What idiots we were."

"You didn't think so then."

"We were children! I still thought Jefferson Starship was groovy."

"Truth doesn't change, hombre," Wasp said.

"That's where you and I disagree," Dave said.

"Why did you oppose me? Did I piss in your cornflakes?"

"Oppose you? Remember Ulthar? I saved you from those things," Dave said.

"Don't mention those cats to me!" Wasp said. He was not joking. "After that. You schemed for my removal. You betrayed me. And for what? You left the Brotherhood. I repeat to you: why?"

Dave started laughing. He laughed for so long that Wasp went from insulted, to angry, all the way to amused himself.

"You thought I schemed against you? I mean, you were a fool at that point. Smoked so much mary you thought you were Thor. You almost cost them everything," he said, taking another drink from his beer.

Wasp noticed how Dave thought of their group as a "them" and not an "us." He was old enough now, and removed enough from his past self, that he could recognize cold truth. Some of the time, anyway. "Yeah, okay, some truth to that," he admitted.

"I didn't hate you," Dave said. "I hated idiots. You were just the biggest idiot."

"Fuck you, too, hombre."

Dave shrugged. "I mean, what was your plan? To take over the Trojan power plant? It would have killed us all."

Wasp had actually forgotten entirely about that.

"Hell, maybe it was my own fault. But why did you care, if you were going to quit?"

"I didn't know I was going to quit. But the heat was coming down. And I got tired of banging my head on the old brick wall. Anyway, we heard from you. Got a postcard now and then. Seems like you did alright."

Wasp grunted a reluctant assent.

"Missing out on the rest of the eighties, all the nineties. You made the right move," Dave said. "Sometimes I still think you were right all along. Just hit the reset button."

"That's not all HE is. He's not just an opportunity for 'reset,'" Wasp said.

"I know, I know. Genesis of all human endeavor or whatever. I've heard your speeches before."

Wasp frowned. He wasn't that predictable.

"You hear about the new guy?" Dave said. "My sources say he got ambushed out in the desert. Not many survived."

Wasp felt good for the first time in days. "Good for her," he said.

"Her?" Dave asked. "Hell, maybe you know more about it than I do."

"Maybe I do."

"Alright, I won't pry. But I hear his pet got loose. Maybe killed him, maybe killed by him. But one of those things free? Terrifies me."

Wasp's good mood dissipated. Another fucking problem, and a terrifying one at that. "That fool of an idiot. They're not *our* servants."

"It ain't like it was in the old days," Dave said.

Both men finished their drinks. They left together. The bartender was still on her phone, and Wasp refrained from leaving any money at all. She wouldn't need it, in a day or two.

They exited the bar together, Wasp close behind Dave. It was now dusk, and the streetlights were on.

"You feel better? Some resolution?" Dave asked. His tone was only slightly mocking.

"You know what? Maybe some things never get a resolution."

"Some things, maybe," Dave said. "Nice that we can agree on something." Wasp ushered him into an alley. Dave walked slowly to the end of it, then turned and faced Wasp.

"You went with Dave, huh?" Wasp asked.

"Well, Dan didn't stick, and I was never a fan of DB," Dave said. "Initial nicknames are the worst."

"You were the best at hiding."

"Until I walked by the wrong bar on the wrong day. Would have figured you for a regular at Shoggoths."

"Not anymore."

"Yeah."

A silence blossomed there, between the two men. Before it became too large and unwieldy, Wasp spoke again.

"Hey, thanks again for Ulthar, hombre," he said. He drew his gun and shot Dave twice in the head. There were no police left in the city; even if there had been, Wasp was already on his bike heading westward before they could have possibly arrived. He had one more mission before the world ended.

CHAPTER 15

The highway was eerily empty; their green van was the only thing on it moving at all. "I don't like this," Maggie said. She was sitting in the back, Kamuks stretched out on the seat next to her. Two swords rested on the other side of her, along with the Elder Sign.

"The good thing," Orson said from the passenger seat—he didn't know how to drive—"is that you brought your dog. A couple of my books hint that they are a weapon against the supernatural." He had a big bag of tangerines in his lap, and a collection of peels was gradually accumulating on the ground beneath him and Maggie.

Maggie scratched Kamuks under the chin.

"You're not a weapon, are you?" she said to him.

"What worries me," Orson continued, "is that the military hasn't closed the roads down."

From the driver seat, Arlo said, "Lucky for us."

"Maybe," Orson said. "But there is an attacker on American soil. How is this not a bigger deal?"

"You know why," Arlo said.

Maggie looked to Orson, then back to Arlo, then to Orson again. No one spoke.

"Well, I don't," she said at last. "And I think it's time you let me know how you know so much about all of this."

Arlo coughed uncomfortably. "I knew she was going to ask."

"You did? What is this? An ambush?"

"Nothing like that," Arlo said. "Only, it's embarrassing."

"You see, our vast knowledge comes from playing too much Call of Cthulhu."

"Fourth edition," Orson confirmed.

"What? What has this taught you about our current situation?"

"Never mind that," Orson said, "It was our starting point, but a couple of things have since occurred to us."

"Hit me," she said. "We still have an hour until we get anywhere, anyway."

"Well, first are the appalling dreams. You've been having them?"

Maggie nodded her head and frowned. "Yes," she said. She dreamed she had died. Cold and bleak shadows had wrapped around her. Was that last night? She couldn't remember.

"We all have," Arlo put in. He ate a tangerine and drove with only one hand on the wheel. They had gone through the farmland and small towns and were now crossing the coastal range. Verdant forests stretched on either side of them. From time to time, far below them, they could see the Columbia River as it flowed out to the sea.

"Well, I suspect we are getting the weakest of the night terrors. That the waves of fear that imbue our dreams here are the weakest. As they spread across the country, the world, they just get bigger and more terrible."

"Like particle physics," Maggie mused. "You're suggesting that most of the world is crippled by nightmares? To the point that the government can't function? The army can't muster?"

Orson shrugged. "Maybe. It's consistent with 'Call of Cthulhu,' and that was basically just him rolling over in his sleep. It explains why we don't see the president on TV. Why the army hasn't blocked the roads coming to and from Portland. Why most of the world seems to be ignoring the end of the world. We are walking the plank, with our eyes wide open."

"I also think the cultists run much deeper than we see," Arlo added.

"I am quite familiar with the cultists," Maggie said. Bonfires danced in her head.

"With this branch, sure. In Oregon, they are kind of ex-hippie/ex-con biker types. But the pull of Cthulhu is strong. There may be high-up officials in the governments dedicated to the return of *him*."

"Governments?" Maggie asked, emphasizing the plural. "Which ones?"

"All of them," Orson said.

They all thought about that for a while. That led Maggie to another thought.

"What do you think about what that ex-cultist said? About

Cthulhu being the font of human creativity?" It had been troubling her more than it should have. "Are we on the wrong side?"

"I mean, what else would you expect a crazy person to say? They have to justify themselves somehow," Orson said. "Anyway, what choice do we have? We can all die. Or we can try to defend ourselves. If our inspiration dies with us, if we become mindless drones.... Well, the loss of Cthulhu won't do much more than we did to ourselves with iPhones and prescription medication."

"I don't want to alarm anyone," Arlo interrupted, "but, speaking of bikers, there is a small army of them on the road ahead of us."

Maggie leaned up and stared out the windscreen. Her sudden nervousness transferred itself to Kamuks, who awoke with a low growl.

"We have to turn around," Orson said. "Take another way."

"Excuse me?" Maggie said. "There are people being chased. Look!"

A lean blond man and a thin blonde woman were circled entirely by riders in dark helmets. The woman held a branch in her hand as she stood back-to-back with the man.

The cultists had dismounted from their mechanical steeds and formed a human chain around their captives. "They have guns," Arlo said. "And they outnumber us."

"Don't be a coward. We can't just leave those people," Orson said.

"I'm not a coward. I'm just afraid," Arlo said, but he pressed down on the accelerator and the van jolted forward.

"Hand me my sword, if you please," Orson said in a very formal tone. Maggie realized he was terrified.

Maggie passed both blades up to the front. The bikers saw them coming but had no time to prepare as the Vanagon barreled into them.

A bike went crashing away as Arlo plowed into it. Orson jumped out, and his gangly body moved with uncanny fluidity. He slashed three cultists to the ground before anyone else could even react. Arlo exited the driver seat with his own weapon drawn.

There had been twelve bikers. Two lay on the ground, and three more clutched at bloody wounds. Maggie slid open the big side door, and she ran for the two victims in the center of the ring.

They looked foreign, paler than even most white people. Both had blond hair and icy blue eyes.

"Come on!" she said. "Into the van."

They looked at her with brief uncertainty and evidently decided she was their best alternative. The three of them fled back to the vehicle.

The remaining bikers, however, readied their pistols, rifles, and shotguns.

Three cultists aimed rifles at Orson and Arlo, who dropped their swords and raised their hands.

"Stop, or we shoot," a woman yelled.

Maggie and the strangers stopped and raised their hands. They turned around and joined the two men as the armed cultists approached them.

One of the cultists said loudly, "Don't kill them yet. They got Vern. Maybe Sandra, too. We want to make it slow."

This was no time to be cute. Maggie brandished the Elder Sign, whipping it from her side. She held it firmly in the air, as she had the night before.

There was no reaction.

"And drop your stick, lady," called a biker.

She let it slip from her fingers, aghast at how disappointed she felt.

"I thought this was supposed to be a super weapon," she whispered.

"Not against people!" Orson said.

"That was embarrassing," Arlo added.

The five of them stood there under the gloomy gray sky, faced with a shooting squad. "Tie them up," the woman cultist said. "We'll take them back to camp. The Accursed is plenty upset, and if we give him new victims—"

The visor of her helmet splintered, and she took two unsteady steps backwards before falling to the ground. Cultists and prisoners alike stared at the fallen body.

Armed soldiers emerged from the woods, shooting with grim precision. A few cultists returned fire, killing two of the advancing men. That was in the brief moments before the cultists died. The men from the forest were equipped with far better skills, experience, and weapons. Anyone near them holding a gun was dead.

"What a relief," Maggie said as she kneeled to collect the Elder Sign. Next to her, Orson also bent down to pick up his sword.

Another shot fired. Maggie looked up, expecting to see another armed cultist, but the shot had come from the soldiers.

Arlo dropped to the ground, his head pulverized like a crushed watermelon.

"What the hell?" Orson screamed. "We're on your side!"

The two they had come to rescue pulled Maggie and Orson toward the van.

"Come on," the man said. He sounded like he had a German accent. "We have seen them in the forest. They are crazy." Orson stood stock-still. Maggie pushed him, and the other woman pulled him, but he just stared at the body of his fallen friend as Arlo's blood continued leaking out upon the pavement. A chunk of his brain quivered five feet away from his body.

More bullets sailed through the air as the soldiers spread out. Orson looked up into the gray sky, his fists clenched. "Elder Ones, grant me your power! Avenge my friend!" He broke free from Maggie's grasp and charged forward. He leaped over a motorcycle and swung his sword in a half-circle over his head.

So many bullets hit him that Orson fell in a couple of different pieces before he even got near his enemies.

From afar, one of soldiers shouted, "I can see the stars shining through their flesh. I will save us all from the bright and twinkling stars!"

Some started singing "Twinkle, Twinkle, Little Star."

Another man kept shouting something about oceans and waves and tides and ducks.

"Kill the asphalt beasts," the first soldier screamed. More guns fired, and the motorcycles were demolished.

"That was fucked up," the blonde woman said. She sounded more turned on than admonishing.

"We are safer in the forest," the man with her said. "Run!"

Maggie called her dog, and they ran for the protection of the pines. They could hear the bullets annihilating the vehicles. "Are they crazy? They really think the motorcycles and the van are a threat?"

The man shrugged. "We saw them shooting trees and rocks while yelling death threats. I don't think you can trust the US Army now."

"You don't have to tell an NDN that," Maggie said. She meant to make it sound jovial, but instead she choked up. Tears poured down her face, and snot flowed from her nose. They walked quickly through the trees.

"Sorry about your friends," the man said.

"They were so stupid," she said, half-laughing, half-sobbing.

"It was quick and painless," the woman said. "Maybe they got better than what is coming for the rest of us." After a small pause, she offered up a timid and forced smile and said, "I'm Anna."

"Cato," said her friend. "We're from Norway."

"Maggie. I'm from here. This here is Kamuks."

Cato bent down and said something in Norwegian, but all Maggie caught was the word "hound."

"Any idea where to go?" she asked.

"None at all," Anna said. "None at all."

"Well," said Maggie, hefting the Elder Sign, "we'd better get started then."

CHAPTER 16

Wasp almost ran out of gas forty miles out of Portland. He'd felt so powerful after his meeting with Dave. Like he was a demigod again. And then this mundane detail brought him tumbling back to earth.

He pushed his bike for a few minutes to a motel, where he spent the dark hours reliving his long-planned vengeance. As the hours passed, the sweetness faded, and he felt increasingly hollow. What was it that Dave had said? "It ain't like it was in the old days." *Amen, brother.* He wondered only now what Dave had meant by "the old days." Thirty years ago, when they were still riding together? Or the *old days*, when humans were just punk-assed monkeys still falling from trees in their sleep?

In the morning he pushed his bike a few miles to one of the last pumps that was still open. Not many people were out on the streets and sidewalks, but the lines at the gas station were longer than they'd been since the seventies. It took him an hour and twenty minutes to get gas, and his mood had soured intensely by the time he got out of there.

He was the only one driving west. Around noon, three men on motorcycles drove toward him. They indicated that he should stop and cautiously watched him.

They weren't nearly cautious enough, though. He shot two of them through their leathers before the third had fully registered what was going on. The fool reached for the rifle on his bike, but caught a bullet in the teeth instead. Two bullets to the head followed, and the road was silent again.

Wasp siphoned some extra fuel from their tanks and claimed the carbine. He couldn't stop chuckling. He had a full tank, extra fuel, and a rifle strapped to his back. Not bad for a morning's work.

He hadn't killed anyone for years and now four people in two days. Well, death was no big deal. Sooner or later, everyone joined the Cosmic Dream.

Wasp started whistling as he got back on his bike. Taking back his kingdom was going to be easier than he thought.

***

He hit a roadblock in the form of a large tree across the highway an hour later. It was guarded by a dozen people all armed with hunting rifles. They crouched next to their bikes, rifles in hand. They were facing away from Wasp, looking west. None of them paid him much attention as he slowed. Wasp knew they were his people because there were six motorcycles parked along the road.

One of them said, "Turn off your engine. They're out there."

"As you say, hombre," Wasp said. He jumped down from his bike and, also crouching, peered over through the needle-covered branches.

"Who's out there?" he asked. "Rambo?"

"Navy Seals, dude. Special Forces. They're killing everyone."

Wasp grunted. "Is that a fact?" He realized the man he was talking to was young, perhaps not even twenty.

The presence of Navy Seals seemed unlikely. No, the new Accursed was more clever than Wasp had realized. He knew this game. Play on the natural paranoia of the cult members. Establish a threat that was vaguely credible but also terrifying. If at all possible, connect it to the government. All of that and you got a unified, cohesive whole—instead of squabbling hillbillies and white trash, which was what the Brotherhood regressed to during the good times. It was a solid move by the new guy.

Only thing was, Wasp had a feeling of danger crawling down his spine. He couldn't see anything, but he thought maybe someone was actually out there.

"Well, there's, what, thirteen of us. Why don't we flank them? Take them in a pincher movement."

The others stared back at him, dull fear reflected on their faces. He realized they were all young. Where were they recruiting from these days? High school?

"They already killed Cameron and Marsha," a girl with black hair and bangs said.

"Cameron was our leader," the first boy explained.

"First thing is, if they were Seals, we'd all be dead. They wouldn't even shoot at us. Just lob a bomb in or come in on choppers," Wasp said.

The girl shook her head. "We've seen them. On the road."

Wasp frowned. "Have it your way. But this roadblock isn't going to stop snipers. They'd just climb trees and pick us off."

"It's worked so far," another of them muttered defensively.

"It was a good plan," Wasp said. "But it will only get us so far." He acted instinctively, taking control from habit. He could reclaim some of his followers.

He liked the idea a lot: turning the Accursed's own cultists against him. *Quid pro quo, motherfucker*, he thought. He only had to dispose of whatever militia these kids had mistaken for elite soldiers. He outlined a plan, and such was his confidence and authority that the young cultists responded without question.

Five of them crept out around the right-hand side of the fallen tree. Six more eased out from the left-hand side. Wasp and the girl with the bangs—Maya—remained crouched. They watched through the pine needles, each clutching a rifle as they surveyed the empty highway ahead of them.

Both sections of the advancing Brotherhood disappeared into the woods. Wasp smiled wanly. They had some woodcraft, despite their young ages. He had to remember how angry he had been that people didn't take him seriously when he'd been that age.

"What now?" Maya asked. Her voice was deadpan.

"If the Navy Seals were here in force, they wouldn't rely on stealth. My guess is there are only a few of them. We'll flush them out, capture them, find out why they are here."

She nodded, a little dubiously. "But what if—"

They could hear the shot. It was followed by two more in quick succession. A long heartbeat later and a cacophony of violence erupted. Men and women screamed. Rifles were emptied. Pistols were unloaded. Trees splintered and cracked.

Then, in less than thirty seconds, silence returned. Wasp's ears, however, still rang from the gunfire.

"What if there are more than you think?" Maya shouted. Her eyes met his, and they were brimming with challenge.

Before Wasp could respond, three of his soldiers returned. They were incoherent with fright, telling tales of being picked off one by one. The explosion of gunfire had come from them. They'd retaliated with everything they had but were not sure if they had even hit anybody.

"What about the other team?" Wasp asked.

They had not seen them.

"Hell," he said. "How far away is your camp?"

He asked it without thinking. It was a mistake.

"Don't you know?" Maya asked him. "Where did you come from?"

"Yeah," one of the others said. "Come to think of it, there aren't many oldies left. And I've never seen you before."

The other team returned just then. Seven of them: the six he'd sent out, and another. The new guy was a blond dude in khakis. Wasp had never seen the man before. His hands were tied behind his back, he was gagged, and his nose leaked blood.

"Who the fuck is this?" Wasp asked.

"Ran into three or four of them," reported the skinny runt named Marc who he'd put in charge. *Always elevate the weakest. They'll respect you and will serve as a wedge against those with more ambition.*

"They had no guns," he said. "Some crazy lady hit Marc with a stick," a bigger boy said. He might have been twenty or twenty-two.

Marc smiled in embarrassment. "Yeah. Right across the back. They got away. We captured this man, though. I don't think he speaks English."

"Didn't you hear the gunfight?" Maya asked them.

Marc looked to her in surprise, to Wasp, then back to her. "Sure we did. Sounded awesome. Didn't you kill them?"

The newcomers realized suddenly that not everyone was there.

"Wait," Marc said. "They're still out there?"

No one had to answer him.

"This is what we're going to do," Wasp said. "Get on our bikes. I know a place we can hole up in." He had no idea of where to go, but he needed to make decisions quickly. In his experience, acting like you knew your shit was generally indistinguishable from actually knowing your shit to the common person.

"The Accursed sent us here," Marc said.

"We're guarding roadblocks along the highway," Maya said. "It's important."

"He didn't know about the troop of Seals out there, did he? If you guys weren't so skilled, you wouldn't still be alive."

"What do we do with this one?" Marc asked. He was proud of his prisoner.

"I'm not sure how that chump got out here," Wasp said. "But he's certainly no Navy Seal. Kill him, and be done with it. It will make *him* happy."

Marc's eyes lit up at the mention of their dark lord. He stood up and whooped. And then his chest exploded.

"*Death is the golden key that opens the palace of eternity,*" a rough voice called out. "But I reckon I'm tired of unlocking that door. Put your guns down." A dark-skinned man with a rifle pointed at them stood on the road, just on the other side of the tree.

Wasp reached for the rock in his pocket.

CHAPTER 17

"We have to go back for Cato," Anna said. She spoke quietly, but her voice was intense. They weren't far from the road where they had been ambushed.

Maggie paused. Kamuks stopped with her. He, ignorant beast, happily believed them to be on a mere hike with some occasional extra running bits. His behavior was strange, however; he kept sniffing the air and growling at nothing.

"We have to," Anna repeated, just as insistently.

Maggie looked for an argument to use, an excuse to summon, but she realized that anything she would say was more simply expressed as "I'm afraid." And that wasn't good enough.

"You're right," she said. A heavy sigh. "He stayed so we could escape. I don't accept that noble sacrifice bullshit. But if we go back, it will probably be to die with him."

"Are you always so cheerful?"

"Something about what has happened since yesterday put a damper on my usual good spirits."

Anna frowned. "I'm sorry. I was just teasing."

"No, I'm sorry," Maggie said. "There's only so much running for my life with no sleep that I can handle."

"You're doing great," Anna assured her.

"You are, too," Maggie said. She breathed deeply again. The scent of the forest, of earth and pine, calmed her. Around them the landscape looked like it did for hundreds of miles. Firs everywhere. Small bushes growing on the brown ground. A few deciduous oaks, bereft of leaves. "What are we going to do?"

"The ones that captured him," Anna said. "I don't think they are the same ones that have been chasing us.'

"How do you know?" Maggie asked.

"They weren't wearing uniforms. They were young, too, university students. And I think I saw a girl."

"Okay. How does that help us?" Maggie asked. All she had seen was guns pointed at her. She'd hit one of the assailants with the Elder Sign, and when it didn't immediately melt him, she turned and ran. They had ducked behind a log and crawled away, expecting pursuit. Instead they'd heard gunshots in the distance.

"Well, they're not insane professional killers," Anna pointed out. "That helps."

"They're not *necessarily* insane professional killers," Maggie said. "That's not the same thing at all."

Anna shrugged. "Still. Uncertainty principle."

Maggie looked at her. "That's not actually how that works. You know that, don't you? Aren't you supposed to be a scientist?"

Anna didn't respond. Her eyes narrowed in concentration. "Get down," she hissed suddenly.

Maggie dropped down instantly. She wrapped her arms around Kamuks to keep him from bolting. A distinctly doggy scent wafted to her. *Sorry, pooch*, she thought. *I gotta get you a bath.*

Someone was walking toward them, and he or she wasn't being quiet. Maggie rubbed her chin as she listened. *We should have gotten farther from the road.*

Anna stood up and ran toward the noise.

"Hey, wait," Maggie said. But then she was up and running, too.

Cato had made it to them. He was bleeding, blindfolded, hands tied behind his back. His knees were scuffed up from repeated falls.

Anna spoke to him in Norwegian and freed first his hands and then his eyes.

"What happened?" she and Maggie asked together.

Cato collected his thoughts for a few moments. His eyes were feral.

"They caught me. I didn't fight, but they," he shook his head, "were rough. They brought me to an older man. He gave them orders to kill me."

"*Faen*," Anna said.

"How did you find us?" Maggie asked. She was concerned he could have been followed. Or was being used to distract them.

"Someone started shooting them."

Cato paused, rubbing at the red band on his wrists where the ties had been.

"The leader seemed to get upset. He ran for his motorcycle. I think he made it. It … it all happened so quickly. I couldn't see, but I heard the engine fade in the distance."

Cato started laughing. "Get this," he said. "The kids laid down their guns. The snipers came forward, but it wasn't snipers. It was sniper. Just one man."

"Some of those guys are pretty elite," Anna said. "My brother was in the, how do you say, *Forsvarets Spesialkommando*?"

Cato, still chuckling, did not register her question. "And he was blind!"

"Excuse me?" Maggie asked.

"Yeah, they all mentioned it," Cato said. "Apparently it was a gruesome sight."

"Gruesome? That is putting it mildly. *Which way I fly is Hell; myself am Hell*," said a rough voice.

They all jumped. Kamuks, however, did not stir.

From the woods strode a nightmare—a brown-skinned man with shoulder-length black hair, wearing what had once been forest camo fatigues; mostly, he was covered in filth. His eyes were ruins, and looked like someone had severely stabbed them with a dull kitchen knife.

"Name's Billy Crow," the man said. "Pleased to make your acquaintance."

"You're the one who saved me," Cato said.

"Just doing my job," the man replied.

"Your job?" Maggie asked. She couldn't stop staring at this man. He looked like a walking corpse.

"US Special Forces," he said. He sounded entitled and arrogant when he said it, and Maggie's empathy faded. She followed the news. She knew the atrocities that Special Forces committed around the globe. But she noticed that Kamuks didn't snarl or growl at him. That, in Maggie's book, was always a good sign.

"I hate to tell you," she said, "but your friends out there do not share your sense of duty."

Billy frowned. "They're not my friends. Not anymore. They went mad."

"Your eyes," Anna said. She rushed to him, reaching into her pocket. Reaching him, she pulled her phone from her pocket and took a few photos. "Hope you don't mind," she said. "I like to collect pictures of fucked-up shit."

Billy Crow laughed. "Don't bother me none. Fucker couldn't get me. He tried. I saw *him*, and my mind stretched."

"Him?" Anna asked.

"Cthulhu," Cato said. "He saw Cthulhu."

Billy nodded. "For a moment. I began to understand something important. Like remembering a dream I'd always been having."

"An epiphany," Maggie said. Images of fish and fog filled her mind. A shadow lay over the memories of her dream, and if she concentrated hard, she could see a burnt skeleton sprawled in a cold fire pit.

That thought gave her the shivers, and she shoved it away.

Billy Crow nodded assent. "Something like that. Like waking up from a lifetime of dreams. Learning to read all at once. But at the last second I saved myself. Broke off a branch and killed the conduit to crazy." He mimed stabbing himself in the eyes.

Cato whistled softly in appreciation. Maggie wondered if she could have done something similar. If she would have to in the future.

It began to drizzle, a cold and merciless fog that left all of them shivering. "Let's get moving," Anna said. "Best way to warm up."

***

"What I want to know is how a creature from Lovecraft came to life," Billy Crow said. It was still raining, softly but insistently. "Either collective belief brought it into existence or H.P. was improbably good at guessing."

They had walked until nightfall. Between them, they had enough woodcraft to start a fire, even in the wet forest. But there was no food. Maggie had seen some mushrooms that looked a bit like Yellow Swamp Russulas, but she wasn't certain enough that she was willing to stake her life on it. Instead, they all tightened their belts and ignored the hunger pains.

"I don't know much about Lovecraft," Maggie said. "Most of what I know came from my friends."

"Cato reads him every year," Anna said off-handedly. "Right?"

Cato's blue eyes gleamed in the firelight. "Not every year. There was a book of Lovecraft in the Bergen library. I loved the cover as a kid, even though it scared me. The first story I read was the one with the man in the castle and the rats," he shuddered.

"Nightmares. It took me years to pick up his books again. But I picked up some Weird Literature again when I was a teen. And you know what I learned? Lovecraft wasn't talking about tentacles and death and insanity. He wanted to show how utterly inconsequential humanity really is. That is the core message. The rest are just trappings: we live in an incomprehensible world, one which we have absolutely no power over. That's why his writing resonates."

"That doesn't exactly help," Maggie said. "We need practical information. What's Cthulhu's plan? What does he want?"

Cato leaned back from the enormity of the question. "We can't know, but anything is possible. Anything. All life could cease to exist, he could devour the sun, or he could sail into space and leave us all alone," Cato answered. "It might be wrong to phrase it in terms of 'plan' and 'want.'"

"But, if he's the source of all creativity?" Maggie asked.

"If that is true, the planet will be a dire place if he leaves. Humanity may well climb back into primordial slime," Anna put in. "It still may be the best of all alternatives," she added.

"Unless we can kill him."

"Yeah. Unless that." Her smile showed what she thought of that.

"Okay, we can't do that," Maggie said. She wondered how well her Elder Sign would do, though. It seemed to be nearly as old as he was. "Can we kick him out of our universe?"

"It would probably help," Cato said. "Don't think it would hurt him much, but at least he would be someone else's problem."

"Great. How can we do that?"

He tossed some moss into the fire and watched it smoke. "We can't. I thought we were just talking hypothetically here."

"Hypothetical doesn't help us. We need to take action. You heard what Billy said?"

Billy Crow nodded in acknowledgment of his name.

"That's actually consistent with what Lovecraft wrote," Cato said. "Our minds cannot comprehend the alien vastness. They break from the strain."

"How does it work? Is it like Medusa? You just take one look and you're a goner?" Anna asked.

"Not exactly like Medusa, I would guess. Look, the physical representation we see here is only a sliver of the whole. The entirety is incomprehensible to us. Imagine a flea in your hair trying to understand the vast organism it is affecting. It's like that, but to a vastly greater magnitude," said Cato.

"Like an iceberg ripping a ship open?" Anna asked.

"That is roughly analogous. In that the damage comes from that which you don't—can't—see. It's not what it does. It's what it is. Cthulhu exists out of our dimension. Theoretically, he could collapse space around you, remove you from the time stream. Space and time aren't constraints for him."

"Theoretically," Anna said.

Cato licked his upper lip once, nervously. "Well, yes. We are in dire need of more data."

"You two are scientists," Maggie said. "Figure it out."

They thought for a few moments. Maggie almost fell asleep. She was exhausted like never before.

"How about sound? What would the aural equivalent of non-Euclidian geometry be?" Anna asked suddenly.

Cato pondered this. "Hmm. Schoenberg, maybe? Twelve-tone technique. Use all twelve tones in the scale."

"Ah," Anna said. "Brilliant."

"Wait, what?" Maggie asked.

"It's a system where all twelve notes are given the same importance. It avoids key entirely. Very different from how we process music now."

"It sounds bad," Cato said. "The musical equivalent of slopping paint on canvas."

"Atonal as fuck," Anna confirmed.

"So, what would you do?" Maggie asked.

"What would I like to do? Maybe create a turntable from eldritch components and play a song," Cato said. "It could disturb Cthulhu greatly."

"*Such sweet compulsion doth in music lie,*" Billy Crow said. He hadn't spoken for so long that Maggie had almost forgotten he was there. It sounded like he was quoting something, but Maggie didn't place it until Anna said something.

"Are you quoting Milton?"

94

Billy Crow nodded, impressed. "Not many people pick up on it."

"I studied pre-Romantic poets for a year at University."

"Are you serious about this magical turntable?" Maggie asked, before Crow could respond.

"It's not magical. It's eldritch," Cato said. "Totally different things."

"And we might be fucking with you a little," Anna said.

"Excuse me?" Maggie asked.

"Yeah, our plan is to go get our prototype gun we left in Portland."

"It is very cool," Cato promised. "We call it the Ragnarök." The way he said it made her think that name was significant.

"What does that mean?" Maggie asked.

It was Billy who answered her. "Twilight of the Gods."

***

They awoke early the next morning and headed east, back to civilization, sweating over hills and carefully balancing across dead logs that stretched over ferny ravines. They splashed through icy creeks and scrambled up rocky precipices. At last, they reached a cliff face that stretched twenty feet into the air. To the left was a deep chasm, and along the right was the ridgeline of the cliff. They were boxed in.

"We can go back," Cato said.

"We are lucky to have evaded the cultists, the army, Cthulhu itself," Anna said. "Beyond lucky. It would be most foolhardy to head back into all that."

"Up this cliff and a few miles away, if we are anywhere close to where I think we are, there are a few small towns. We can call for help or beg a ride once we reach them," Maggie said.

"A shower," Anna said. "I feel so dirty."

Maggie studied the rock wall for a few moments. It didn't look entirely impossible. "I've been bouldering up and down the Coast Range. I can maybe do this, even without rope and chalk. I assume our military friend here can climb, even blind? Don't you guys practice all that stuff blindfolded?"

Billy nodded. "When climbing, you have to empty your heart of fear. If you have fear, you will fall."

"Another Milton quote?" she asked.

"Nah," he said. "Just something I heard on television."

"What about you two?" Maggie asked, turning to the scientists. "Do you know how to free solo?"

They shared a hearty laugh. "We're Norwegian," Anna said. "Climbing is what we do on our rest days."

"What about your dog?" Cato asked.

"He's a crag dog," she said sadly. "He comes on a lot of my climbs with me. But he can't climb that."

"You will leave him behind?" Anna asked.

Maggie stared at each of them in turn. "Oh, god. Don't make me do this."

CHAPTER 18

Wasp liked to think of himself as a chill guy. When he had to react with violence or be a tough guy, it was only because of how unreasonable other people were. Such was not an inherent facet of his own personality.

Part of him, buried deep down, understood this to be a fiction. But deeper still, at his very core, he grasped that this fiction, and others, were essential parts of his continued existence.

Thus, he found his exasperation troubling on a very existential level. He had barely escaped with his life and had not even managed to track down Luther, the architect of his trouble and pain, or so part of him not buried very far down at all had come to believe.

His rock, his source of power, had done nothing when that soldier had confronted them. When he touched it, it had not responded in any way. Wasp had been lucky to get away, and he wondered what had happened to the Brotherhood who surrendered. The rock still worked to some extent. He could feel things around him, sense deep truths, but the eldritch energies it held were no longer his to command. Without it, Wasp had no plan, no course of action. He was utterly listless.

Wasp had gotten back to Portland to find a city overrun with cultists. The normal citizens of Portland seemed to be gone. Locked sleeping in their houses or packed up and fled back to California or Michigan or wherever they had come from, he didn't care to find out. Most of the remaining cities in the world were openly worshipping Cthulhu. Wasp smiled. A city of cultists was a city he could establish some power in.

The old Wasp could have, anyway. The man who had ridden up from Cusco, camped in jungles, bartered with bandits, defied corrupt border officials. He'd fancied himself brave.

He knew otherwise now. Bravery wasn't acting tough when you carried power in your pocket. That was, well, he didn't know the word. Posturing, perhaps.

Wasp walked to Pioneer Courthouse Square. It had once been called Portland's living room, but these days it was Portland's

BDSM tattoo parlor and sex dungeon. Starry-eyed street kids and suit-beclad businessmen alike were joined in the cult of Cthulhu. It was not as wild as some of their isolated meetings, but still. But still.

Some stood on a giant chessboard and read from virtual *Necronomicon*s on their smartphones. A pretty young tattoo artist, her skin nearly black with ink, had set up shop above the steps and was giving tentacle tattoos to any who wanted. Plenty did. Many danced in various states of undress to weird, cyclopean rhythms they heard only in their heads. Some, perhaps many, were not fully human. There were beings with frog faces, fish gills, shark teeth, membraned fingers, fur and antlers and other less identifiable things, too.

"When they said to 'Keep Portland Weird,'" Wasp muttered, "I don't think they meant it like this." He regretted being alone whenever he thought of his funniest lines. "Story of my life," he muttered again. "How are there so many cultists? These people would have scoffed at inclusion in anything other than socially-approved niceties just a week ago. Now they tattoo tentacles on their titties?"

He knew the answer even as he voiced the question. Unlike every other cult leader who had ever operated, Cthulhu had access to a unique recruiting technique. Dreams. Maybe that's what dreams always had been, a way for the Ancient One to speak directly to humanity. Explained a lot.

Wasp watched the new cultists exult in their newfound freedom. "Party away, freaky friends, party away," he said. It was as good a way as any to spend the last hours before oblivion.

A commotion over by the chessboard caught his attention. A group of men in leather jackets, carrying rifles, shoved the new cultists aside. Wasp recognized one of them. It took him a few moments, and then it clicked.

The bouncer from the beachside bar. The day he'd lost his position as Accursed. It felt like a lifetime ago, but was really less than a week. Shit kept happening faster and faster.

Wasp stood up. If the Accursed had his men here, he could show up any time. And Wasp no longer felt up to the challenge of fighting him. Not when he knew the power of R'lyeh was no longer his to command. Not when he knew that a lone sniper had been too much for him and his team of young cultists.

As Wasp turned, he felt something cold and hard shoved into his back.

"Going somewhere, old man?" a voice asked. The muscled young man had shaved his goatee, and his face was red and splotchy with burn marks, but Wasp knew who it was. The Accursed held a pistol pressed close into his back, and the older man slowly turned around.

"You don't look so good, Luther," Wasp said. "Didn't your parents ever teach you not to play with matches?"

Luther laughed. "You'll wish you had suffered only as much as I have soon enough, I can assure you of that." There were two cultists behind him, bearded men carrying rifles. One was drinking a cup of Stumptown coffee.

"The Great Lord is coming," Wasp said. "Are you ready?"

"Of course," Luther said. "But that's none of your concern." He waved his hand and said to his two men, "Take him to the hotel. Search him. Bring me anything unusual you find. You know where I'll be?"

"The welcoming party," said the man on the right. His beard had streaks of gray.

"Hawthorne Bridge," the other repeated. He was younger, taller, skinnier. The weak link, Wasp reckoned.

"Don't kill him yet," the Accursed said. "I want him to see the master's arrival."

It was indeed fortunate that he was such a chill guy, Wasp thought. Otherwise being led at gunpoint to imprisonment in the last couple hours of his life would be a real bummer.

CHAPTER 19

Portland was a subjugated city, and it sat meekly awaiting its triumphant conqueror. Flanked by raving men and stygian monsters, Cthulhu was mere hours away. Anna and Cato had barely reached their hotelmotel before they collapsed from exhaustion. That morning their group had found the empty town of Jewell and had stolen an abandoned car. Maggie dropped them off at Sentinel Hotel and continued on with Billy Crow to pick up her father, with plans to meet in the eastern part of the city that evening.

There was still no sign of action from the government. Not a helicopter in the sky or even police in the streets. Wi-fi was working again, and Anna checked Twitter and Instagram and Facebook, and saw that all around the world there was almost no online activity. No new posts; it was as if everyone in the world had fallen asleep at once. The lack of breakfast posts and selfies wasn't unwelcome, she had to admit.

Their room had been undisturbed. Cato worked on assembling the R99 while she showered. Anna went and raided a store for coffee and snacks. The shops were abandoned, shelves full of food, cash registers bursting with money. Neither of these commodities were currently much in demand.

Anna spent too long looking around the mart. American food all had so much sugar in it, but she found some peanuts and sandwiches still refrigerated. She stuffed as much coffee as she could into a plastic shopping bag. She and Cato both feared to sleep.

There was a dirty, tenebrous energy in the streets. It reminded Anna of the Roskilde. On the last day of that music festival, gangs of drunk people found empty tents and lit them on fire. Only they weren't always empty. And tents weren't the only things they burned.

This was like that but much worse. She wished her brother was there to help her. Was he okay? What were her mom and dad doing? Were they sleeping through this? Her attempts to call home had been unsuccessful. Anna pushed it all from her mind and concentrated on the present.

She knocked on the door.

"What is the password?" Cato asked.

"*Noe lukter vondt*," Anna said.

The door opened. Cato grinned at her. "That actually would be a good password."

"Or we could just say anything to each other in Norwegian."

"Yeah," Cato said. "Or that."

He sat back down on the sofa. Before him was a myriad of parts.

"How is it coming?"

He shrugged. "We didn't really think anyone would want to see the prototype," he said. "But another hour—two, tops—and I should have something ready."

"Cato," she said, suddenly serious. "If you have to, could you? You know?"

"Kill someone?" Cato said. "I hope so. I have hunted moose before."

"A moose is not a human," she said.

"I know," Cato said. She realized he was still wearing his dirty moose jumper. It was ripped and muddy and had dried blood on it.

"You should clean up. Eat some food. We won't meet Maggie until tonight. We have time."

Something banged hard on the door. Anna and Cato stared at each other.

"Were you followed?" he asked.

"There are people out there. I didn't turn invisible, if that's what you mean."

"I think you were followed," Cato said.

The banging intensified, and it mixed with shouting and wild chanting.

"Shit!" Cato said.

"Did you say an hour?" Anna asked.

"Maybe thirty minutes," Cato said. He dove into the tools and pieces. He had a long way to go. She still wouldn't have recognized a gun in all that mess.

"Got it," Anna rushed to the bed and pulled the mattress off. She dragged the bed frame over to the door and pushed it against it. Her arms were wiry and her back was chiseled muscle, and it was no sweat to add the minifridge and wardrobe to the barrier. The banging did not stop, but it grew muffled.

Cato was completely silent, lost in his task. Anna went to the window and glanced out. They were three stories up. "Fuck it," she said. She sat down on the mattress and ate a bag of spicy peanuts and drank a cold bottle of Starbucks latte.

The door splintered. "How are we doing?" she asked.

Cato looked at her helplessly. He shook his head. More pieces of door fell away.

"Finish later," she said. She emptied her suitcase of clothes, dumping them on the floor, and brought it to him. Together, they threw the parts and tools into the suitcase.

In the hallway outside their room, someone howled.

"To the window," Anna said. "Bring the R99." She grabbed the bags of food and coffee.

Cato glanced down dubiously. "It's a long way down," he said. "We could try to jump to that ledge. But it is not—"

"We're not going down," Anna said. She kicked at the window, breaking it open and then kicked at the frame until it fell out. "We're going up."

The bed slammed down. Four women stood in the doorway. They were bloody bacchanalian Furies. One, with hair as red as fire, howled. The others shouted, "Ia! Ia!"

Cato scrambled out the window and pulled himself up to the next floor. Anna was right behind him. The suitcase and bag slowed them, but they managed to evade the fury of the howling cultists.

Below them, the streets were emptying. Everyone still alive in Portland was making their way east, toward the river. Most were human, but others were woodland creatures crawling from the dark forests. People with badger faces or porcupine backs. Men with antlers. Women furry like raccoons or skunks. No one looked up and saw the Norwegians purchased on the side of building.

Slowly, as quietly as they could, Anna and Cato climbed up to the fifth story. This was the last floor. Above them, only the roof awaited. It was not difficult to climb onto the windowsill and grab the crenellation. Cato went first, and then Anna handed him the suitcase and food bag. She climbed up and joined him in stunned silence.

Even in Oslo, a five-story building didn't provide commanding views, but the few true skyscrapers in Portland were scattered. Thus, they had a clear view of the creature emerging from the west.

"*Faen*," they said together.

Cthulhu was as big as a mountain. He strode across the land like a champion, like a conqueror, like a king.

Like a god.

Anna stared. It was difficult to see any details clearly. The body was human, lethally skinny, and there were long bat wings behind it. Could Cthulhu fly? She tried not to look at the face, but irresistible pressure left her with no choice. Her mind filled with soft singing. There was so much beauty in the world. So much greatness. She raised her arms into the sky to better absorb the divinity.

Something punched her in the stomach, and she fell to her knees. Her body gasped for air even as her mind still reeled from the raw sight of Cthulhu. After a few moments, she realized Cato was next to her. The cold roof pressed into her skin.

Checkered patterns and green ovals swam in her eyes. Slowly, she could focus on the four chairs that surrounded a table. She reached up and touched the leaves of the plant above her. They felt fake and plastic.

Cato peered into her face. He was close enough to kiss her.

"What happened?" Anna asked. She could see more clearly now. The roof was perhaps ten meters long and four meters wide. A table was set with red napkins in the middle. On the other side was a door that led to the staircase and the conventional way of gaining the rooftop.

"I'm sorry," he said. "But I was shouting your name. You didn't hear me. You couldn't stop staring."

"What about you?" she asked. She took a deep breath. Reality was beginning to feel a little more real.

"My glasses. I lost them when the cultists caught me. I can see just fine without them, but not far away. I saw a blur and shut my eyes."

"Hindsight is—" Anna said. Before she could finish, a door from the stairs burst open. The four women who had battered their way into their room rushed through. The red-haired woman had a fire axe in her hand. The three other women with her, all brunettes, had fresh blood smeared around their mouths.

The flame-haired woman raised a bloody finger and pointed it toward the two Norwegians. She raised her head to the sky and barked like a dog. Her companions surged forward.

Anna scrambled up, but Cato grabbed her shoulder and pushed her back down. "Don't even try it," he said. "*It* is much closer."

Cato reached down to the suitcase and came back up with the Ragnarök in his hands. It looked more silly than terrifying. Most of it was a disc which was held below by two gun butts, giving it the appearance of the Starship *Enterprise*. But Anna knew it was a devastating weapon.

"It's finished?"

"You were out for a while," Cato explained.

"What are you waiting for? Shoot them," Anna said. The women were mere meters away now.

Cato raised the gun at them but hesitated.

The women were so close Anna could see a pimple on the leader's forehead.

"I can't!" Cato said.

Anna grabbed the weapon and fired. The Ragnarök fired a thousand microblades every second, and Anna, in her panicked fear, held down the trigger for at least five seconds.

When it was done, there wasn't much left of their attackers. Blood, some chunks of flesh, and fine pink mist in the air.

Cato stared at her like she was someone he had never seen before.

"How could you?" he said. The ground shook.

"It's not like they weren't going to do the same to us. You do what you gotta," Anna said. "Moose aren't even threatening your life," she added, and immediately regretted it. The earth shook again, much more heavily.

"People aren't moose," Cato said. They were thrown to their knees by the force of the next tremor. That ended their argument. "Get down. We can't be on the roof for an earthquake."

"It's not an earthquake," Anna said. Without closing her eyes, she could still picture that throbbing body, those magnificent wings. "It's Cthulhu. He has come for us at last."

CHAPTER 20

It wasn't hard for Wasp to break free. They had marched him to a hotel room and stood outside the door. Both the middle-aged man and the skinny kid were new to a game he had been master of for a long time. And a hotel room was not a prison cell.

He felt a little bad about killing them, but his guilt was assuaged firstly by the rifle he now carried in his hands and secondly by the rifle strapped to his back. Wasp carefully made his way down the stairs, but he needn't have bothered. The hotel was empty. The streets were empty. Portland was empty.

Wasp walked down to the Hawthorne Bridge. The mighty bridge sagged from the weight of the bodies on it. The welcoming party appeared to include every person left in the city and quite a few who were not, strictly speaking, entirely people. Wasp found a bench on the riverfront and looked through the scope on his rifle.

Smoke rose, marking the trail of the Great One as he made it to the city. A horrid mountain of destruction—the most destructive force this land had seen since the glaciers had carved out canyons and valleys in the last Ice Age.

They had raised the middle section of the Hawthorne Bridge, the part that moved up so that tall ships could sail up the river. The Accursed stood alone on the raised section, shining in his moment of triumph. Wasp was having none of it.

He knelt down on one knee and took four shots in quick succession. Luther's body went still, then tumbled down past the bridge and into the dark water. It landed with a splash. A stentorian groan went up from the collected cultists.

Wasp threw both rifles on the ground and reached for his stone, his fragment of the UnderCity. No power seeped into him. He did not have time to be disappointed, though, for at that moment Cthulhu arrived. The mighty master of all reached the city that had called him so many years ago.

Ten thousand worshippers sank to their knees, genuflecting in abject obeisance. Cthulhu paid their worship no heed. His tentacles descended into the mass of people. Some crashed through the bridge with eldritch force. The whole structure shook. More tentacles wrapped up the puny humans, brought them to his slavering maw. The bridge groaned as metal stretched and twisted in ways it was not meant to. Wasp looked up; he started laughing and couldn't stop.

Even the most fervent cultists panicked now. The crush of humanity was far too dense to allow easy escape. And there were so many tentacles—moving with a slithering, blinding speed, far more quickly than mortally possible.

The Hawthorne Bridge fell into the Willamette River. No humans were left on it. In the thirty seconds since the Great One had appeared, he had eaten or crushed the tens of thousands of mortals who had come to worship him. Cthulhu hammered the bits of the bridge that were sticking out until they were submerged.

Wasp watched with an intense feeling of *déjà vu*. He had seen all this before. He had seen Cthulhu wade up the river, had seen himself shoot down a man on the bridge. It had been in his dream of meeting Cthulhu, the dream from which he'd woken up with the R'lyeh stone clutched in his sweaty fingers.

It was that stone, he guessed, that was keeping him sane while watching the Great Old One. That, or he was completely insane. The insane probably didn't know they had gone mad, did they?

Wasp stopped worrying about it as his consciousness slipped away from him; it rose into the air like a bird.

He watched Cthulhu rise out of the river and smash down the iconic Portland neon. He watched as Cthulhu flattened the Bank of America building, reducing it to rubble in mere seconds. The many-tentacled one rambled up the street, smashing food carts and buildings and parking meters and smart cars alike.

The counterattack came suddenly and without warning. Wasp had been wrong; the city was not empty of all, save cultists. Office towers and restaurants alike were full of hitherto unseen Special Forces.

They didn't waste bullets on their mountainous foe. A team cracked open a window from a tall office tower, and they fired bazooka after bazooka into their eldritch enemy. Another unit ran in with flamethrowers, creating extensive infernos. On rooftops around the city, pairs of Special Forces armed with Stingers set up tripods and fired them at the Mountain That Moved. Tanks rolled out from parking garages, and the sky was filled with enough drones to blot out the sun. There were other weapons there, ones that Wasp didn't know, but he did not doubt it was some heavy ordnance, indeed.

The cacophony was deafening. Missiles screamed through the air. The scent of burnt flesh filled Wasp's nostrils. He wondered how they managed to see the Great One without going insane.

They fired enough to reduce a mountain to rubble.

Cthulhu struck back. With one incredibly gargantuan hand, he picked up a ten-story building that was brimming with gunmen, like a boy plucking a flower, and flung it over his shoulder. It soared in the air and landed out of sight, miles away. An enormous tentacle crushed the flamethrowers so utterly that only red splotches were left on the ground. He lumbered forward and crushed the tanks under foot. His wings created a hurricane that blew drones back and soldiers and weaponry off the roofs on which they were perched.

Many soldiers were blown as far as the river. One landed feet first, with a sickening thud, just a short distance from Wasp. Bones stuck out messily, and blood flowed from the man's ruined body. Wasp approached him, eyes caught by a Star-Trek-like device on his eyes. Wasp picked it up gingerly and let some of the blood drip from it before looking into it.

He could see satellite images of the area. Those who had the device were hooked up to a street view via satellite; they could see everything, but virtual renditions of it. Wasp turned toward Cthulhu and saw a crudely-rendered illustration. It looked like it was from a children's cartoon.

Pretty goddamn fucking smart, he thought grudgingly.

As Cthulhu's former high priest of twenty years, Wasp's connection to Cthulhu was still strong; as Wasp saw and understood what was happening around him, so too did the entity known as Cthulhu. The Great Old One stomped toward Portland's iconic statue of a woman kneeling with trident in hand. The statue was thirty-five feet tall and weighed several tons, but Cthulhu ripped her from the building and flung her high in the air.

The statue blasted up like a rocket and almost instantly disappeared from sight. Moments later, the GPS went out. It took

Wasp a moment to piece it together. And when the idea did creep in, sideways-like, he refused to listen to it, but there was no other explanation: *Cthulhu had taken out the satellite overhead.* Wasp had no idea how high up satellites were, but that was pretty damn incredible.

Now operating blind, the remaining soldiers scrambled back to their parking lots and buildings. The drones swarmed in. They aimed for nothing other than to hit the great monster. Cthulhu batted them away by the hundred, smashed them out of the air, blew them away with his wings, but plenty managed to hit.

Something chattered in his ear about HMX explosives. Wasp took cover behind a tree. He could see the drones hitting the gargantuan Cthulhu, could see them exploding with a terrifying force. But no chunks of flesh blew apart and no blood or ichor leaked out. The Great Old One seemed to be entirely unharmed.

The sky was clear of drones.

Cthulhu had killed or eaten most of his cultists, but a few still haunted the city. They emerged now, shooting at the Special Forces, and mostly earning quick deaths. Cthulhu smashed with uncaring precision. The areas he had wrecked looked like no buildings had ever been there. Other than the concrete on the ground, there was no sign of humanity's presence. It was like he was erasing the city.

His earpiece sputtered. "Air strike coming in. Advised to seek cover."

Wasp ran and dove into the river. Even as he did, several jets shrieked toward Cthulhu, missiles plowing through the air.

The water was black and cold. The visor was torn from his head. He sputtered and splashed and after a few minutes found his way to a ladder on the side of the river. Wasp climbed up from the Willamette, dripping like a muskrat. The sky was empty; no planes yet soared, though smoke plumes throughout the city hinted at their fate. More of the city was gone. Erased from existence.

Cthulhu approached another building, one with a vaguely Turkish onion dome on top. He hit it so hard it was reduced to dust and atoms. Something happened, because all at once, muscled, camo-wearing men were fleeing as though the devil himself was at their heels. Wasp watched them, and then found another dead soldier. He put the visor to his eye. Still static. The earpiece was crackling, though, and Wasp brought it closer.

—uclear Strike is incoming. All friendly forces have two minutes to evacuate.

In the northwest part of the city, near Chinatown, several choppers brimming with fleeing soldiers rose and darted off. Wasp watched them go. He shivered in the cold. There was a piece of flesh caught in his bandana. It was impossible to tell what part of a person it had once belonged to.

A whistling sound alerted him to the incoming missile, and he suddenly found that he did not yet want to die.

"Oh, Cthulhu," Wasp prayed. "Your power is unmatched on this space pebble we humans call home. Save me, unworthy as I am, if you deign to."

Cthulhu reached up with several tentacles and pulled the nuclear missile into his mouth. Wasp closed his eyes. Nothing happened. He waited for several seconds, unable to believe his continued survival. And then he fell to his knees, water dripping from his clothes and hair, but filled with joy and relief and adoration.

"Oh, thank you, mighty Cthulhu!" he cried. "I was a fool to doubt your power."

In his mind, a wet, ancient voice answered: ***YES, YOU WERE.***

Wasp passed the fuck out.

CHAPTER 21

There was a note patiently waiting on the counter. It read, in her father's semilegible scrawl, "Gone to town to stock up. Back tonight. Let's talk. DAD."

Maggie felt terrible. He must have waited all day yesterday. She was a bad daughter, and she resolved to be a better daughter in the future. If there was a future.

She showered and changed into much-needed clean clothes. As Billy showered, she toasted three pieces of bread and added cheese and sliced cherry tomatoes for the world's most basic pizza. Clean and satiated, she sat down on the couch to wait for Billy. She wasn't sure about the soldier in her dad's shower. She disliked army guys almost as much as she disliked cops, but his presence made her feel safer. He was a killer, and she was glad he had asked to come with her.

Her thoughts turned to Arlo and Orson and how miserable their deaths had been. They had attacked gun-wielding men with swords. That worked in movies, but not real life. The idiots.

She thought of her father. She thought of her pup, left panting happily below the rock wall they had ascended. There was so much sadness in the world; there always had been. Maybe it was best to stop fighting and let Cthulhu win. Tears rolled down her face. Without meaning to, Maggie fell asleep on her father's couch.

Did she dream? Maggie never knew, but flames crackled in her subconscious.

She awoke to the sound of gunfire. Her mouth tasted rotten, and sleep nuggets crusted her eyes. It was dark outside. Billy Crow knelt next to the door, his rifle in hand. He was dressed in her father's jeans and a work shirt. They were of a similar size, she realized.

Maggie thought a lot of things at once. *What time is it? I'm late to pick up the scientists. Where is my father? How long did I sleep? Why is Billy at the door?*

Glass shattered as bullets shot through the house from outside.

"What's going on?" she asked.

"Stay down," Billy Crow said. "There are armed men outside."

Maggie rolled off the couch and onto the ground. The entire house was dark. "It is so late. Why didn't you wake me up?" she asked in a low voice.

"Wake you? There was an earthquake three hours ago, and you didn't stir."

"Three hours? Earthquake?"

"Be quiet," he warned. "They're coming back."

She listened. Perhaps the crunch of gravel sounded faintly from outside, but it might have been her imagination. She slowly crawled toward Billy.

The long-haired soldier poked his rifle through a broken window next to the door. She heard his breath stop as he focused all his senses on listening.

Billy fired once. A body dropped, and someone swore loudly. Now she certainly did hear gravel under feet, as people scrambled back away from the door.

"Move," he said, rolling away from the door and behind the thicker walls. Maggie followed him.

A hail of gunfire hit the door, splintering it. Pieces of wood fell away, littering the ground with broken shreds.

"There's still three of them. Maybe four, if I only winged that one," Billy Crow said.

"Who are they?"

"Does it matter?" he asked. "They have guns, and they want to shoot us."

Maggie thought about it. "It might."

"My guess is cultists. Or looters. They're not organized. Not brave. Not smart."

"You can hold them off, though?"

"Negative. I can't watch the back door. And I'm down to my last shot."

"With armed bandits out there?" Maggie said. "Excuse me?"

"I had plenty of bullets yesterday," Billy Crow said. "Turns out I had a lot of bad guys to shoot."

"Don't you Special Ops guys always have a backup plan?"

"There isn't exactly standard operating procedure for the end of the world."

Maggie lost her anger and surprise. She'd known it already, of course, but hearing him say it made it feel so much more real. *The end of the world.* It really was. Everything she had ever hoped for, all of her dreams and sadness, her favorite books and the reality TV she loved to hate, it was all meaningless. Everything that made her a person didn't matter at all.

"We can't stay here," Crow said.

"My father will come back."

"If he does come back, do you want it to be to your dead body? Leave him a note."

"Good point," she said. She thought for a moment. Her pickup was parked in the front, right next to the gunmen. "Okay. I know a way out. We can go through the backyard, hop the fence. There is a track that leads down to the river. It's a little rough."

"I can manage," Billy said.

Maggie scribbled a quick message on the note her father had left. *Find us in Hood River*, she wrote and stuffed the paper into her pocket.

More bullets hit the house. Not content with just the door this time, the bullets sprayed through everywhere. Glass shattered as windows broke open. Maggie dropped down and pressed her face into the carpet. She thought of Orson's skull, cracked open, and trembled in fear.

Something creaked. "They're on the porch," she said to Billy. He muttered something about a claymore. "I gotta check the back," he said. "Take my rifle. Fire it out the window."

"I won't hit anybody," she said. "I've never fired a gun in my life."

"It doesn't matter. Aim for a car or motorcycle if you can. They will think I am shooting. It will buy us a little bit of time so we can escape. Keep your head down."

She did as he said. She poked the barrel through a broken window and fired the last bullet into the darkness. The gun kicked back more than she was expecting, bruising her shoulder.

Outside, she saw the shadows scatter back again. There were more than three, she thought, but it was hard to tell.

She set the gun down and grabbed the Elder Sign. Through the kitchen and past the pantry, Billy Crow sat with his head pressed against the back door.

"We good?" he asked.

"I hope so," she said.

He unlocked the door and silently opened it. They made their way through the yard, past the doghouse, and slowly over the fence. Neither moon nor star had pierced the vale of clouds above, and the darkness slowed them down.

"It's so dark," Maggie said, then realized for Billy it was always dark.

"*What is dark within me, illumine*," he responded.

She slipped the note into the doghouse. There was a chance, however small, that Leonard would look there. He didn't know Kamuks was gone, anyway.

A tense minute later, they were free. She knew the path down the hill, had known it since she could walk. It would lead down to the historic highway, where they could hike a few miles into Hood River. She grabbed Billy's hand. "Come on," she whispered. "Be careful; it's steep."

He pulled his hand away. "I can do it."

A powerful light brightened the driveway in front of the house. Maggie glanced back only for a moment. The strong light hurt her eyes, and she looked away, temporarily blinded, but she had looked long enough. She had seen the man ablaze in the beacon. A man tied up, surrounded by armed gunmen. A helpless prisoner.

Her father.

CHAPTER 22

Anna had gone missing. Together, they had crept down the stairs, emerged onto empty streets, and then while Cato was peeing on the side of a building, Anna had simply disappeared. The plastic bag full of snacks and coffee lay abandoned on the street.

At that moment, the Great Old One rumbled into the city. Cato didn't mean to, but Cthulhu took up the entire sky, and the Norwegian looked directly at him. His mind melted like a wax crayon on a hot day. All at once, he remembered every dream he had ever had. Images of the beach and giant waves and deep caves and scruffy goats and a thousand others filled his mind. Cato fell to his knees, his hands clasped to his head, in mental anguish.

He could no longer tell what part of his life had been dreams and what part had been real. He no longer knew what real meant. Even the very distinction between dreams and reality seemed utterly childlike and pathetic. His eyes were open, but he could not see the world around him. All he could see was a portal of ghastly proportions, one full of rugose and dreadful creatures.

Monstrous greyhounds, lean as a whisper, padded through those gates, while above them were crows that had mole faces and vulture wings and yet were none of those things. Shifting bubbles slithered over crawling squamous serpents. Behind it all, radiating malevolent power, was something goatlike and utterly frightening.

His consciousness fought back. It overwrote the blasphemous portal with an image of a moose. The creature was strangely blocky, and not until he concentrated did he realize it was the moose his grandmother had knitted. The moose on his jumper.

From that single building block, Cato reengineered the world. Matter was put back into distinct parcels—chairs here, tables there, trees over yonder. He remembered who his family was, what his name was. He remembered that in 1985 *a-ha* had released "Take On Me" and created what was still one of the greatest music videos of all time. And with that influx of entertainment information, that most human of creations, his mind burst with favorite bands and movies, with famous actors and stark novels, visionary directors and lonely painters. His mind was whole again.

He opened his eyes, panting and sweaty. Cato was careful not to look up at that which filled the sky. The city was full of the sound of guns and rockets and death and war. It sounded like World War 3 had started while he was dreaming. There were no people within sight, and he still held the suitcase with the Ragnarök in it, but being out in the streets made him feel too vulnerable. His legs were weak and shaking, but he slowly regained his feet. Just a block way was an enormous bookstore. It seemed a safe place to rest until he could find Anna.

Anna. He had seen Cthulhu for less than a second, and it had almost ruptured his sanity. Anna had stared for a long time, ten seconds or more. What had happened to her?

***

What happened to me? A small part of Anna's brain protested, but it was an impotent protest. Anna walked down to the river, called there by a sweet song. It filled her like a drug, and she needed it like an addict. What *it* was she didn't even stop to ask.

The Willamette River was murky and sludgy, full of chemical runoff and sewage overflow. Anna didn't even blink as she dove in. The water was dark, but down, far down, was the prize she had come to claim.

It glistened like a pearl, even from meters and meters away. Anna swum down seemingly forever. She realized she wasn't even holding her breath. Instead, she breathed the water as effortlessly as she had formerly breathed air. The rational part of her mind began to calculate how that could be possible. Perhaps H_2O separating in her body?

Her hand reached the glowing white piece of rock. She grabbed it and felt eldritch power suffuse her. Her appearance didn't change, near as she could tell, but inside she was completely altered. He Who Slept had blessed her with great power.

Energy flowed through her. She could see not just the world around her, but how it was imbued with cosmic implications. River. Words were such frail constructs to contain the immense things they tried to capture.

Anna shot forward, up through the water, high into the air, and landed on the east side of the river. Her hands twitched and jerked in a series of kabbalistic motions, and her voice, high and hoarse, screamed out in a language no human had ever spoken and none had heard for eons.

The Drowned One stood across the river, battling men. Anna basked in his eldritch power for a moment. Never a religious woman, she suddenly understood what those deluded fools had always felt. It was an immense moment, one that filled her with wonder. And then, someone shot her. The bullet passed through her heart and out the other side.

Anna laughed. She was unharmed. Her hand ripped itself from her arm and sailed through the sky, trailing tendrils of dark energy. The sniper, peeking out a warehouse window five buildings away, found a hand on his throat. His windpipe was crushed. The building had once been a game store, and it was marked by flaming wings and a halo. Two more soldiers rushed from the ground floor of the building. They shot their rifles at Anna with frightening accuracy.

Bullets tore through her body, but no blood flowed from them, and she felt no pain. Her hand flew out the window. It stretched and grew and tore apart and darkened until it was five distinct columns of throbbing energy. Two slammed down upon the soldiers. One of the men shot at the descending darkness; the other fled from it. Both died.

The tendrils swirled and collected around Anna's arm, and her hand reattached. She jumped high in the air to land near the closest body. It lay in a tangle of broken arms and legs but was still warm. Anna lay her hands on it and drew its heat, its life force, into herself. The holes in her body closed. She felt healthier than ever.

A whistling sound caught her attention. A bomb soared down from the clouds, but the Almighty swallowed it. She had the sense of it detonating somewhere very, very far away. Across the river, standing alone, a grungy-looking man wearing a faded blue bandana tumbled to the ground.

Something niggled her mind. There was a man she had traveled with, someone she had known for years. His mind still resisted the magnificence of the Dreamer; his eyes remained closed to the reality of the Drowned One's grandeur. She had to share her message with him. She had to save him.

She had to find Cato.

CHAPTER 23

"You sure it was your father?" Billy Crow asked.

"I have to go back. They'll kill him."

"If they aim to kill him, you going up there ain't going to stop them."

"You think they'll kill me, too?"

"Maybe." Billy shifted his weight. "Maggie, look, I've been on both sides of this. Well, more the other one than this one. Your father is bait. They spent the better part of the last hour trying to kill you. You go back, and you're both as good as dead. I'll tell you that for nothing."

"I leave him to die, and what is the point? I mean, we are chickens running around with our heads cut off. We're dead already, and we just don't know it. Cthulhu is going to kill us all or eat the sun or some other esoteric incomprehensible nonsense. If I have a few days to spend, it will be with my loved ones or not at all." She surprised herself with her own vehemence.

"Not to put too fine a point on it," Billy said.

"Well, you asked."

He inclined his head toward her. "Reckon I'll make my own way down there. Rather take my chances with the road."

"I understand. Turn right, walk for three or four miles, you'll reach town. Not sure anybody is still there, but—"

"I understand." He reached for her hand. "Good luck." He turned and ambled down the path.

"Billy," Maggie said. He stopped walking and cocked his head. "Good luck to you, too."

She strode back up the trail. Two men searched the backyard. When they saw her, they jumped over the fence and grabbed her. One man punched her in the stomach. The other ripped the Elder Sign from her hand.

The air driven from her, Maggie couldn't explain she had come back on purpose. Or maybe they knew. She realized that maybe Billy had been right. They dragged her back, around the house.

Several people with guns stood in the driveway. There were a handful of motorcycles and a Jeep. It was mounted with a green spotlight, and in front of the light her father was tied up. He looked old and tired. "We got her," called the one who had punched her in the gut.

"And look what else we got," said the one who now had the Elder Sign.

A woman with a blonde undercut and wearing army surplus camo snatched it from his hand. "It has returned to us. Weren't there some more? It wasn't just her?"

One of the men shrugged. "Who cares? We got what we came for."

She turned and looked at Maggie for one intense moment. She shrieked and slapped Maggie in the face. Tears sprung in Maggie's eyes.

"I saw you there the night you stole this. Injured the Accursed. He won't ever be the same again."

"Excuse me," Maggie said. "It wasn't me trying to burn you alive. I came back to you of my own free will. Let my father go."

"That isn't how it works," the woman said. "I think you mistake who gets to make demands."

"We should kill her, Lauren," the man who had punched her said. "I heard about what she did out there. Kill them both, and be done with it."

"Their lives are not for us to determine," Lauren said. "It is for the Drowned One to say. We will bring them back with us."

The man frowned, his bloodlust unsated, but he did not further question Lauren's decision.

"How many did you lose before I got here?" Lauren asked one of the men.

The man shook his head, frowning. "Jacob. Kevin. Martin. All dead. Just me and Tyler and Jeremy survived. And Tyler got shot in the arm pretty good."

"It will have to do," Lauren said. "It took too many of us too long to reclaim the Sign. We may have missed the Homecoming." She clapped her hands. "Alright, dudes. Saddle up."

***

The ride back to Portland was dark and cold. Maggie could not speak to her father; both were gagged and tied to the frame of the

Jeep. Uncomfortable as she was, Maggie fell in and out of sleep. The long nap earlier had not caught her up.

It must have been midnight when they got to Portland. There was a large bonfire on Mount Tabor that the Jeep and motorcycles headed up to, through the fir-lined streets of East Portland.

The fire was much bigger than she had realized. Most of the trees that had grown atop that once volcanic hill had been cut and added to the fire. Smoke rose into the sky like a beacon, and it smelled of campfire and burning trees for miles and miles. It was an end-of-the-world kind of bonfire.

When Maggie had driven through Portland that morning, it had seemed empty. But there were plenty of cultists up here—hundreds, if not thousands. The sight of so many cultists gathered around the fire should have made her recollect some disturbing memories, but presently she was beyond caring. The only thing keeping her going at this point was habit.

That, and a slowly growing hatred for the particular cultists who had captured her. As they untied her father, one of the men drove his fingers up her father's nose. He twisted his fingers and jerked them out. Leonard's nose leaked blood weakly. The bewildered expression in his eyes almost broke Maggie's heart.

Maggie was furious. She struggled against the bindings, but they held too tightly. The same man untied her from the frame of the Jeep and scooped her up in his arms as though it was his honeymoon.

He jumped down, and they followed Lauren and the Elder Sign toward the fire. Maggie wondered about Lauren. She looked to be about twenty years old and probably until recently had been a server at Stumptown Coffee or Voodoo Doughnuts. Could be one still, if it weren't for the long black dagger in her hand. How had she gotten a position of authority?

Maggie had been up to Tabor a few times in her life. Usually the lights of Portland flowed like the sea in all directions around the mountain, but tonight there was only primeval darkness. It looked as though electricity had not even been invented. It looked as though light itself had barely been conceived of. To the west loomed a shadow of the mountain that moved. The few stars that remained in the sky shone with a sickly wan light that made

Maggie feel ill if she stared at it for too long.

They reached the circle around the fire. Flakes of paper-thin tree fell from the sky like blasphemous snow. The man carrying her put her down and whispered into her ear, "I'm going to gut you like a fish."

Just ahead of them, Lauren stopped.

"What are you doing here, old man? Where's the Accursed?" Lauren asked.

"I am the Accursed," replied the man. "The Once and Future King to boot."

Maggie recognized that voice. She bounded forward and almost tumbled into Wasp.

He looked bigger than she remembered. The pupils of his eyes had tripled in size; the mania in his eyes had increased beyond measure. The bonfire behind them cast shifting shadows on his face.

He stared at her like a drunk person who keeps blinking as he tries to place someone he thinks he should know.

"Ah, I do know you." Then he turned to Lauren. "Why is she gagged? You had your chance to kill her days ago, at Shoggoths. Now there is no point. Too late."

His wild eyes shifted to Maggie, and he spoke with the enthusiasm of a ten-year-old. "Did you see our Drowned Lord? The Lord of Sea and Storm? I have always believed, always. But today he spoke to me. I am a feeble worm but—."

Lauren interrupted. She held up the Elder Sign. "The Accursed sent me to reclaim this."

Wasp nodded diplomatically. "Good. Give it to me."

"Where is he?"

"He stands before you, humble in the shadow of the Almighty."

"Where is Luther?"

"Alas. He has joined the Sleeping One in the other realm."

Lauren's face turned so pale that the change was visible even in the firelight.

"No," she said. "You couldn't have. You couldn't have." She ran at Wasp then, swinging the Elder Sign. He did not react quickly enough to dodge her, though he raised his arm to ward off the blow.

The Sign shattered his arm as though his limb was made of balsa wood. From elbow to hand, it twisted and fell at an unnatural angle. Wasp roared in pain. Suddenly, he held a pistol in his left hand. Lauren was lost in fury, and she swung at him again. Wasp shot three times. Two bullets pierced her chest, and her body fell to the ground. It all happened so quickly that only those near the combatants had even noticed the fight.

Wasp stepped up and kicked Lauren in the ribs with enough force to break them. She did not move, did not register the kicks at all. "Throw her on the fire," he said. "Let her ashes fill the sky. It can only help our summoning ritual." Cultists scurried to do his bidding, heaving her body deep into the fire. Wasp turned to march away.

The cultist who had carried Maggie to the fire nudged her. "What about her? And the old man?" he asked.

Maggie tried to speak, but the gag still held.

Wasp didn't even look back at them. "Kill them, fuck them, fight them, all the same to me, hombre. It's the end of the world, and I don't care."

CHAPTER 24

She could not die. She could fly through the air with the ease of slipping into a dream. Her hands were spectral weapons. But she could not find Cato. All day long she had ignored the increasingly powerful summons from the Drowned One and had looked for her former partner. She felt on some level that the nuclear bomb had hurt *him* more than it had appeared on this plane. Perhaps he was not truly damaged, but the wind had been taken away from him for a few hours.

Anna tried to use that time well. She had many powers now, but clairvoyance was not one of them. The afternoon waned, and though she had searched the hotel and the restaurants nearby, she had not found Cato. She kept getting attacked, first by crazed members of the Brotherhood, and then by the few surviving soldiers barracked in town. She killed them all.

Once Anna learned how to raise her opponents from the dead, however, the challenges ceased. Her cadre of bloated death warriors followed her will implicitly. She merely had to think a command, and they would do it.

Once she had a score of servants, she sent them lumbering through the ruins of the city. She sat on a statue of an elephant and closed her eyes; she could see other realms and the horrific creatures warring in them. It was like having every movie ever made in her mind, only with creatures and places few humans had ever imagined or seen. She remained motionless all night, her mind both shrinking from and growing into the hideous visions that beset her.

By the next morning, a dozen of her minions had returned, and she gave up on any more finding her. She instructed the dead things to lead her. They shifted uncertainly in place, not capable of advanced thought. Anna frowned and swung her hand at one. It stood three meters away, but her arm stretched like a tentacle, narrowing into a shadow.

She hit it so hard that it burst into a million dead cells and skin flakes. These spores rose up into the city, and as Anna concentrated, they drifted north along the main street. Anna hurried. The Slumbering One had spent the night healing, and she sensed another of great power on the east side of the river. Time was running out for her to collect Cato.

***

Cato was not the only one who had taken refuge in the bookstore. There were at least a dozen other people there. Most had been there for some time. Not long after Cato arrived, they'd blocked the doors at front and back by dragging the immense shelves in front of them. That left quite a few windows as vulnerable points, but there was no avoiding that.

The bookstore was huge. Locals called it a city of books, and they were hardly exaggerating. There were maps up front to help customers navigate the four stories. There was a café on the ground floor. Cato wandered around the store, aimlessly at first, but gradually with a purpose. He went to the gold room and grabbed some books on Cthulhu. He then made his way upstairs to the rose room, where he selected a few books on mythology. For good measure he found the red room and perused the military section. At last he had collected ten tomes, which he stacked on the suitcase holding his doomsday weapon. A group of five people bade him goodbye. They could not stand waiting anymore and wished to see what was happening in the city.

Cato was too surprised by the recklessness of this action to advise against it. Besides, they were adults and capable of making their own decisions. He sat down in a surprisingly cozy corner to browse the books he had found.

His investigative skills were lacking, however. Cato had always been a good student, but he found it impossible to maintain focus. Too much was going on outside the walls of this wordy fortress. He worried about Anna, though in his heart he had to accept that she was probably dead. Was there a way to return to Oslo? Did any of his friends or family yet survive? Were they merely asleep? Did they even know about any of this?

There were too many variables; too much was unknown. He wondered if the Ragnarök could hurt Cthulhu at all, but rather doubted it. Insanity lurked for any who even looked at the monster.

When Maggie had dropped them off that morning, he hadn't

expected things to go so bad so quickly. The city was smashed to bits. Their plan of meeting again was up in smoke. If Maggie yet lived, he hoped that she had gotten as far away from here as possible.

He didn't mean to fall asleep but had been pushing himself too hard. His eyes closed. Some hours later, his eyes opened. It was dark outside, middle-of-the-night dark. A half-moon ducked in and out of clouds. Cato was still tired, and he stretched out on the floor and fell into deep, dreamless slumber.

The pale sunlight of morning woke him; he felt hungry and stiff. Breakfast, perhaps even coffee, beckoned, but first things first. After a few stretches, he sat down in front of the pile of books.

"*Skjerp deg*," he muttered, forcing himself to sharpen up as he opened a book called *Elder Signs and Ancient Ones*. It was quite fascinating, written by an early twentieth-century anthropologist named Sasha Kosović who claimed to have infiltrated a real cult of Cthulhu in New Zealand. Interestingly, it was made up entirely of rich Europeans. Cato skipped past the boring sections about cult dinners and what port they drank and read about the Elder Sign.

Kosović claimed it was covered with extraterrestrial microbes. This is what gave it its power. This was all heard secondhand, as this cult didn't actually possess the Elder Sign, and only one or two of the higher-ups even claimed to have ever seen it.

His eyes hurt from so much reading in a foreign language and without his glasses. He wished he had brought another pair. Cato skipped a little more ahead, past more descriptions of fire-lit nights and snarling dogs and brandy sipped, to something called "The Revelation of R'lyeh."

The cultists speak of a city hidden under the sea, a lost Atlantis of cyclopean proportion. Some claim it is really Atlantis, that Socrates himself was a cultist of Cthulhu, and it was for this crime of worshipping the Ancient Ones that he was sentenced to death.

Cato skipped ahead again, his finger sliding down the page.

My dreams last night imply that R'lyeh is not a slumbering city hidden beneath the sea. Mortem ipsum ut morietur. What I realized upon awakening, when my consciousness and subconscious joined in harmony, is that R'lyeh is nowhere at all.

A shadow fell over him. Cato looked up to see Anna. He jumped up, heart filled with happiness, but even in those first few seconds he knew something was wrong.

"I have found you," Anna said. Her voice came from under the sea.

"Where did you go?" Cato asked. He stared at her more closely. Her pupils were enormous. Her skin wriggled as though things crawled through her body. And even standing in the sunlight, her body seemed wrapped in shadow. "How did you survive?"

"Oh, Cato!" she said. "I didn't merely survive. We were so wrong."

"We were?"

"The Slumbering One is not our enemy. He has come back to save us. To lead us."

He wanted to think that she was joking, but seeing her wild eyes and hearing the altered tone of her voice, there was no fooling himself.

"I have spent too long looking for you," Anna said. "Come with me."

"I'm not going back out there."

She looked at him blankly. "You must. He wills it."

"If he wills it, then I'm really not going out there."

She screamed. Her hand shot out and stretched to quadruple its size. It struck a four-meter-high bookcase with enough force to knock it over.

Cato swallowed in fear and surprise. *"Fy Faen,"* he said. "Where did you learn to do that?"

The way she looked at him reminded him of the first woman whose heart he had broken.

"Cato, come with me. Accept him. He is all. He is everything. I can't protect you otherwise."

Cato glanced down at the Ragnarök. There were five cumbersome books on it, and the suitcase was latched shut. There was no help there, even if he could bring himself to shoot her. "Who says I need protecting?"

"The US Army dropped a nuclear bomb here this afternoon. The only reason you are still alive is because the Lord of Dreams saved your life."

There was no arguing with her, but he pushed on.

"I suppose that had nothing to do with his own survival?" he asked.

"That was never in question. Our Lord cannot be hurt. You yourself said it. He is not of this place."

"He is not of this time?" Cato asked, an idea slowly forming in his head.

"Yes, exactly." She smiled innocently. "You begin to see. I knew you would."

"There are others in the bookstore. Can they come with us?"

She shook her head, annoyed at the stupidity of the question. "I killed them already. You are the last."

"You killed them?"

"Well, my men did."

"You have men?"

She cocked her head in thought for a second. "Not men. It sounds strange to call them zombies, but maybe that's the closest word."

Her powers are bizarre and vile, Cato thought. *Though what else would you expect from an alien god millions of years old?*

"Your zombies? Anna, does it strike you as strange that yesterday morning we were running for our lives, and now you have zombies and shadow hands?"

"We weren't running from him. Only running from lost souls who could not comprehend his magnitude. It matters not. Death is no misfortune. It's simply a return to the Great Dream we all share. A drop of rain falling back into the river."

"Well, this raindrop is staying here," Cato said. Her words were infecting him, though. He wanted to give up this futile resistance. To have purpose, and to serve a greater power.

Anna perhaps sensed the effect her words had, and she reached for his hand. "Come with me. He is leaving Portland soon."

"And going where?"

Her smile got bigger. "Everywhere!"

CHAPTER 25

Wasp disappeared into the darkness, and the cultist leered at her. Maggie felt his hairy hands groping at her body through her t-shirt, and she wished with all her heart she could simply die right then and there. Wood smoke burnt her eyes. She glanced down to the ground to avoid the smoke and saw *it*.

"Jeremy," one of the others said, "what do you want me to do with this one?"

"Kill the old man," the cultist said. "She shot three of us at her house. I'm going to kill her slowly."

The threat to her father infuriated her. Maggie didn't even think. She reacted with inspired violence; she head-butted the man holding her, hit him hard enough that he stumbled back into the fire. Maggie ripped her hands free and grabbed the Elder Sign from where it lay momentarily forgotten on the ground.

She advanced on the cultist behind her father. He moved backwards, hands up.

"It's alright, lady," he said. "You can have him."

"Are you okay?" she asked her father.

He was still gagged, but he mumbled something and swung his eyes wildly to the left. Maggie turned to look far too slowly.

Jeremy leaped from the fire and kicked her in the chest with a karate kick. The back of his shirt was on fire. Maggie reeled backward. She backpedaled, but swung her hands out to catch her balance. Her right hand still clutched the Elder Sign, and the top branch caught Jeremy in the temple. He crumpled to the ground like someone had hit his off switch.

A few cultists who had watched clapped and hooted their support.

Maggie ignored them and untied her father. He stared at her with wide eyes. "I had no idea you were so violent."

Maggie frowned. "I wasn't. Come on, let's go."

There was a myriad of cultists on that mountaintop, all enjoying the apocalypse in their own way. None deigned to stop the pair of them as they found a steep, cracked pair of steps and made their way down, away from the hazy bonfire into darkness.

They had not gotten halfway down to the streets below when Leonard stopped. He raised his hand, silently beseeching Maggie to stop. He panted loudly. They were on a paved trail flanked by tall pines on either side.

"What's wrong?" she asked.

Leonard paused and then pulled up his shirt. Maggie stepped forward and stared. It was not dark enough to hide the dark blood that oozed from the bullet hole in his side.

"What happened? Are you okay?"

"I'm fine," he said. "Got shot when that blonde woman went crazy."

"You're not fine, Dad," Maggie said. The wound looked really bad. She felt his back and realized the bullet remained lodged in him.

"I just need a little rest."

"I'm going to take you to a doctor," she said.

"You know that's not going to happen."

"I'll find you one somewhere. You're going to be fine," Maggie said. He was right, though. The hospitals would be empty, their doctors dead or departed.

Her father could hardly hobble, so she supported his weight as best she could. It was difficult to do so with the Elder Sign in her hand, but she persevered. He was light, lighter than she would have guessed, but still she struggled. By the time they walked past an eerily glowing tennis court and onto the street, Maggie's calves were quivering, and she could feel her back was damp and sweaty even in the cool night. The half-moon was intermittently casting light, but now was behind a bank of gray clouds.

"Magpie," her father said gently.

"No," she said. The street they stood on was empty and dark. Abandoned houses leered at them with orange flickering from the fire on top of the mountain behind them. From westward, toward the river, a dog howled mournfully.

He ignored her. "Leave me here. Get to safety."

"No," she said again. "That's not going to happen."

"You can go find help," he said. "Come back for me."

"Excuse me? You think I am going to just leave you here? You can't die. You're my dad."

"Run," he said.

Puzzled, she looked at him.

"Run!" he said again, much louder. She glanced up and down the sidewalk, not sure which way he wanted her to run. To their left, behind a hedge, was an old house. The street was on their right, but it remained dark and empty.

The air swirled around them, filling with bubbles of darkness. They coalesced into something writhing and misshapen. Tendrils squirmed and flexed ten feet above them, looming like snakes poised to strike. Maggie had the impression of neon eyes and open jaws full of sharp teeth, but the creature was in a state of flux. It was in a hundred places at once—before them, above them, around them, surrounding them. The peril in the air around them felt almost tangible, and the thing itself, whatever it was, throbbed with horrid color.

Maggie stepped in front of her father and brandished the Elder Sign. The shadow beast seemed to withdraw. Was it the same creature she had encountered at the cult gathering at Steens Mountain? Or the same kind of creature, if there could be more than one of its kind?

"Get back," Maggie cried.

A ribbon of darkness swung down at her. It avoided the Elder Sign and hit her hand. It stung with the venom of a thousand rattlesnakes. Maggie screamed and dropped the Elder Sign. Her hand immediately swelled, doubling in size from the protoplasmic poison.

Maggie fell to her knees. Pain filled her body and overwhelmed her mind. She could only see sharp jagged edges of red. She reached out for the Elder Sign but could not find it. Now, her hand was utterly numb, and the numbness spread up her arm and through her body.

Her flesh benumbed, her mind coated with dark frost, Maggie pitched over. Her head smacked into the ground. Her father shouted something, and vaguely the parts of her mind not yet frosted with gloom thought he sounded joyous.

Something wet and warm intruded on her oblivion. Words appeared in her mind, anchoring her sanity: tongue ... licking ... shaggy ... friend ... pooch ... *Kamuks*.

Warmth flooded her as her consciousness fell back into her body. Her dog stood before her, roughly kissing her face with his tongue. Her body could not move; she was pinned down by tendrils of concentrated darkness, but her mind had returned from the brink.

The squirming mass stretched and surrounded them like a dome. A tendril reached for her face. Kamuks turned and growled. It was a feral, Jurassic growl, and Maggie felt the hairs on the back of her neck rising even though she knew it was in her defense.

The tendrils increased the pressure on her wrists and knees tenfold. Maggie screamed.

Kamuks snarled and leaped at the darkness. Maggie's father picked up the Elder Sign. He threw it into the air at a dense cluster of eyes and mouths. The Sign stuck into the quivering shadow mass and stood still in the air.

The creature screamed with the pain and rage of long eons. The pressure on Maggie dissipated, and the fear that filled the air slowly drained away. The bubbles and sharp teeth and glowing eyes retreated in on themselves, like a sink full of water easing down a drain. And then the monster was completely gone, erased from the world. The air felt warmer, and the smell of Portland and pines returned to them.

The Elder Sign quivered and then fell from the sky. It landed on the other side of the shrubs, next to the empty house on their left.

Maggie stood up and rushed to her dad.

"Are you okay?" they asked at the same time. She gave him a big hug and then turned to her dog. "How on earth did you get here?" She remembered hearing howling and wondered if it had been him.

Her father slumped, and she helped him sit down.

"I think I need a doctor."

"I haven't taken first aid since high school," she said. "I wish I knew what to do."

"It's not your fault."

"There must be a hundred videos on YouTube," she said. "But I don't suppose the internet is still working. Power is out everywhere."

"If only there was a way to learn other than the internet," her father mused.

She smiled. "You're right. We need to find a place with a lot of books."

He nodded. "Just what I was thinking. You should go to a bookstore."

The oddest feeling hit her. "Haven't we been there already?"

He narrowed his eyes. "Are you feeling okay?"

She shook her head. "I must have dreamed it. I thought we'd been to a bookstore in the air."

"Well, you never know with Powell's," her dad said. "There are always more everywhere you look."

"Maybe we should go to Powell's," Maggie mused. "But not yet. There is a Walgreens close to here and a Freddies. We can find some alcohol, clean your wound." Her mind continued the thought. "And we can find a shopping cart, and I'll push you to Powell's."

"Maggie. That's not a dignified way for a man to travel."

"Do you prefer dignity or life, Dad?"

He shrugged. "I'd prefer it not to be an either/or choice, I suppose. But I'll come with you."

"Good," Maggie said. "Just wait a second. We can't leave without the Elder Sign."

She walked over to where it had fallen but stopped mid step and hissed. The Elder Sign had defeated the monster, killed it or driven it to another realm. But in doing so, it had shattered into a dozen pieces. They were scattered over the yard and scarcely visible in the moonlight.

"What's wrong?" her dad asked.

"I don't think we should have done that," she said, bending down to collect the warped and fragmented pieces.

"Done what?" her father asked.

She thought about it. "Survived, I guess," Maggie said.

"That's morbid," her father said. "But perhaps very true."

"Dad? Do you ever dream that you're already dead?"

CHAPTER 26

"Everywhere," Anna said. "We will go everywhere."

Cato stood transfixed, a moth to her flame. He shut his eyes and breathed deeply, but still her presence engulfed him. He was drowning in her.

A loud crashing noise from downstairs jarred them both. Anna turned her head, and the spell was broken. There were sounds of people screaming and dogs barking.

Anna bent her head in concentration. "How came she to this place?" she said, and her voice sounded to Cato like it belonged to someone else.

The barking grew louder. Anna turned to face away from him. Cato didn't think. He dove for the suitcase—Anna's suitcase—and pushed the books off it. It took precious seconds to unclasp it, and he felt, rather than saw, Anna turn her attention back to him as he did so.

"What are you doing?"

"Something I'll regret the rest of my life," he said, and he fired the Ragnarök into her through the suitcase. The minidiscs tore through her, and her body jerked from the impact.

She did not disintegrate, however. Whatever eldritch forces she possessed kept her body together. No blood flowed from that myriad of wounds. The power of the R99 knocked her back two meters, but she threw her hand up, and a shadow formed in the air. Some of the discs stopped in the air, but the Ragnarök fired a hundred thousand discs per minute. Even her powers could not stop all of them.

The assault continued. Her face drooped and melted like wax under the sun. Tears ran down his face as he watched her disintegrate.

"I came to save you," she said. "Don't you see how useless this is?" For the first time, she sounded like herself. Cato kept shooting her. "We are all just aspects of the Slumbering One. Humanity itself is just one tentacle of his power. Join me in the Cosmic

Dream …" her voice trailed off, and her body fell to the floor. She didn't so much disappear as morph into the things around her. The matter that had been Anna was now floor, now a bookcase, now a copy of a book called *H.P. Lovecraft: A Life*.

The ground rumbled, and the entire building tilted at least five degrees. Every bookcase still standing slanted over and fell to the ground. The air filled with dust and the smell of old paper.

Cato wiped at his eyes with the sleeve of his jumper, then grabbed the book by Kosović and the R99. He passed over the spot where Anna's body had died. No sign of her remained, but there was a strange crystal sitting on the ground. It thrummed with urgent need. He reached for it, and then thought better of it. It was better to leave the unknown well alone.

The ground shook again, and Cato barely kept his balance. A tentacle crashed through the side of the building. The tentacle was as big and as thick as an elephant, and Cato wanted no part of the being that it belonged to.

He bounded down the stairs in two steps and sprang forward. The main room was a mess; everything had crashed to the floor. But the exit was straight in front of him, only twenty meters away.

Cato looked up at the door to see if it was still blocked and skidded to a stop. A gray -haired man stood topless, his skinny arms raised into the air. On the other side of him, where Cato could not see, someone was bent down with her head near his waist. To her side was a mangy dog that Cato stared at.

The dog whined at him in greeting.

"Kamuks?" he said. Somehow, this was the most surprising thing he had seen all day.

From in front of the old man Maggie peeked out.

"Cato?" she said. Her expression matched the confusion he felt.

There was a wrenching sound as the entire building groaned. Tentacles as thick as oil tankers wrapped around the outside, and with a violent motion the entire building was lifted into the air. Edges of the building crumbled away, and Cato had to duck as books flew by. Shelves crashed to the floor.

The floor tore away beneath them just in front of Cato. Books and shelves and periodicals and toys and cash registers alike all poured through the hole and down toward the ground. Maggie and the old man grabbed onto the front door. The dog scrambled on unsteady paws, but the slope increased, and he began to slide down to the hole.

They were raised ever higher into the air. Already they were taller than the tallest buildings.

Kamuks scrambled toward his master. The desperate scratching of his claws on the wooden floor was a haunting sound.

"No!" Maggie cried. She slipped away from the door and slid down the now almost-forty-degree angle toward the gaping hole. Cato started to charge forward and then thought better of it.

Instead, he pointed the Ragnarök at the hole in the ground and fired. As always, it was silent and had no kickback. Thousands of discs shot into the creature that carried them.

A snake-sized tentacle whipped in from outside and smacked Cato on the back of the head. He stumbled forward, losing control of the gun and the book he held in his other hand.

The building shifted again, tilting the other way. Kamuks and Maggie slid back toward the old man at the front. The book caught on an upraised piece of floor; Cato and the R99 went spilling toward the hole. Something went tinkling past him as he grasped at the slick floor.

Cato reached the R99 just as it was about to fall. He threw it over the hole and hoped it didn't hit Maggie or her dog. Then he slipped through, just catching onto a pipe with his right hand.

The fifth floor had already ripped away, and pieces of the bookstore crashed to the ground. He didn't want to, he didn't mean to, but Cato looked down.

Beneath him was a whirling maelstrom of energy and chaos. He squeezed his eyes shut and only saw more clearly. They were above the clouds and only halfway up the creature that carried the bookstore. It was so vast that it dwarfed every other living thing. The tallest trees that had ever risen from the earth were ants to this monstrosity. Apart from the impression of immense size, however, Cato was less sure about what he saw.

Cthulhu himself was indistinct, an oil painting of blurred lines and hazy distinctions. Cato had the sense he was emaciated, jagged bones and harsh edges. The great creature was lean as a greyhound. The tentacles were not like those of an octopus or squid but rather tendrils emanating like rays from the sun.

The wind blew hard, and the pipe was wet with his sweat. Cato's hand slipped, and he tightened his grip. He brought up his other hand and clutched the pipe. His muscles were hard as iron, but the rock he was used to clinging onto was considerably more stable than this. A heavy book hit him in the back of the head, and dozens more flew out, leaking a trail of discarded literature behind them.

Cato focused all of his energy on the strength in his fingers. Butterflies danced in the pit of his stomach as the sheer drop imposed its enormity on his mind.

Two hands reached down and grabbed at his wrist. "Hang on," Maggie called.

She pulled at him with unexpected strength, and Cato scrambled up, back into the building. The bookstore, whether through motives inscrutable to them or sheer happenstance, was more or less level now. Cato shivered from the sky's coldness that had settled into his bones.

"Are you okay?" she asked.

"I think so," he said, but he couldn't stop shivering. She wrapped him in a hug for a long minute. The connection to another human helped him as much or more than the borrowed body heat.

She broke away. "I have to finish helping my father. I pulled the bullet out, but ..."

"I can help," Cato said. He still had a bullet wound of his own, after all. He introduced himself to the short, brown-skinned man.

Twenty minutes later, Leonard was bandaged and resting next to Kamuks.

Cato secured the R99 and went to look for his book. Maggie followed him.

"*He* is carrying us somewhere, isn't he?" Maggie said.

"I'm afraid so."

"How is the building still together?"

Cato pointed to a partially crumbled wall on their left. "See that steel girder? The building must have a steel frame. And I suppose being supported by thousands of tentacles doesn't hurt."

"But why?" Maggie asked. "In my dreams I saw a bookstore in the sky. How is this possible?"

Cato saw his book at last and grabbed it.

"What is that?" Maggie said. "We have some books on first aid already."

He showed her the book *Elder Signs and Ancient Ones.* "Something I found upstairs. Seems to be relevant to our situation, even if most of it is made up."

"I don't understand."

"It doesn't matter. I don't think I can explain it, anyway. But I think we have a talisman that is valuable to Cthulhu. I suspect that is why he is keeping us alive. Carrying us somewhere for his purposes."

"I'm not going to serve him." Maggie said.

"I don't think we have much choice," Cato said. "Unless you want to take the world's longest swan dive from one of the windows." When Maggie stared at him seriously, he grabbed her arm.

"Not a serious suggestion. So, what happened to you yesterday? Last I saw, you were with the blind soldier."

"Billy escaped. I was captured by the cultists, along with my dad. They brought us into Portland. We got free."

"I see," Cato said. He sensed there was a great deal she was leaving out but did not press her. They made their way back to her father and dog, who were by the front doors, which were still barred shut. By mutual assent, they tried not to look out the windows.

"After my father was wounded, we were attacked by …" she trailed off and looked at her father.

Leonard shook his head with a little smile that indicated his lack of knowledge.

"By a something," Maggie said. "Something alien. Kamuks appeared from nowhere, scared it, gave us time to kill it."

Cato nodded. "I read something about that in this book. I suspect it's a reason why man domesticated dogs in the first place. This book, okay, it was written by a crazy person. But he hung out with Cthulhu cultists a hundred years ago."

"What did he say?" Maggie asked.

"Wolves and bears and other animals were apparently made by a race called the Yithians as they warred with, well, something bad. I'm not sure what. Maybe Cthulhu or aspects of him? Anyway, dogs were one of the most successful weapons they made. Their lack of conscience perhaps renders them immune from the alien powers of the old gods. They were made to bond with masters, made to confront the horrors of the Eldritch Ones."

"That makes as much sense as any of the other answers I've thought of. Which isn't a lot, mind you."

"It isn't."

"Cato," Maggie said. "I have been afraid to ask, but I have to know. Where's Anna?"

He looked away from her brown eyes.

"She's dead. I think she's dead."

Maggie sighed. "It's time like this I wish I was religious."

"Well, we saw god today," Cato said. His joke was half-hearted and not funny, and Maggie did not laugh.

"We did see him," she said, "but we aren't insane."

Cato cocked his head. "The Elder Sign, I suppose."

Maggie reached into her back pocket and withdrew a handful of strangely stretched fragments.

"I don't know if it still works," she said. "The Elder Sign. It's broken."

She looked crushed. The gears in Cato's mind spun and then clicked into place. *Maybe.* "Do you mind if I take a look at it?" he asked, reaching his hand out to her.

Before she could answer, the sound of planes and helicopters and guns echoed through the room. The entire bookstore shook and bullets flew in. Without warning, the entire structure dropped. They hurtled to the ground far, far below.

CHAPTER 27

Billy couldn't believe his ears.

Commander Plover was the highest up in Special Forces, on par with the director of the CIA. The man dined with the president and entertained foreign royalty. Pigeon, the ill-fated leader of the first Cthulhu strike force, had been several steps beneath him. And now Commander Plover had taken personal control of the military and set up base in a big brewery in Hood River.

Billy had walked right into the camp. Plover had personally collected and debriefed him. Billy told him everything he knew. It wasn't much, but Billy had more firsthand knowledge than any soldier living. In turn, he learned of the two failed attacks since the one led by his own unit. One happened halfway to Portland, when two divisions had been wiped out to a man. Then, just yesterday, Plover had planned and executed an elaborate attack from within the ruins of Portland itself. It had involved soldiers equipped with satellite goggles, state-of-the-art technology, and a nuclear strike.

And yet the score currently read: US Army, 0; Cthulhu, 3. But men like Plover didn't climb the ranks only to give up when things looked bad. Plover sat in a command tent in Hood River made entirely of right angles. This, he told Billy, kept most of the insanity and dream force away. If that was sanity, Billy Crow was pretty sure he didn't want to know what insanity was.

Cthulhu knew they were there. He was coming for them, aiming to eliminate the last of his enemies.

The United States Army wasn't used to losing, and Plover did not try to hide his anger. His next attack would use natural geography against their colossal foe. Billy got the sense that, win or lose, Plover's career was over, that a lot of the weapons he was deploying were not approved and had perhaps even been stolen.

Now Billy sat in the command tent, in the back but still allowed in as a nod to the ordeals he had survived, while the commander spoke to his subordinates and aides. Time was running out.

"That's right. We have a thousand FX Raptors," Plover told the assembled men.

Billy had a buddy that flew an F22. They were loaded with missiles, carried up to eight in fact, could fly almost up to Mach 2, and were capable of ground attack, recon, and electronic warfare. But what an FX was, he didn't know.

An unfamiliar gun was pressed into his hand.

"What's this?" he asked. He didn't even know who he was addressing. Now that survival seemed more than the faintest of possibilities, he regretted his blindness. There had been little choice at the time, though.

"The AA12," a woman said to him.

"Assault shotgun? Ain't gonna do squat against *him*."

"It's not for him. There are approximately two hundred twenty, two hundred thirty, insurgents coming up the highway."

"So. Bomb them."

"We will. The AA12 is just in case. This one fires frag grenades. Be careful."

He didn't like her tone, but the gun felt good in his hand.

Plover shouted, "Professor Swan has got the Black Knights. I want hundreds of them crammed so far up that squid's ass that we all eat calamari tonight."

Billy whistled. Black Knights were remote-controlled tanks, with immense cannons and deadly machine guns. A valuable weapon for confronting their ancient foe.

"I want ADS all around the entire perimeter," Plover continued. "If he does break through, I don't want him to hit our nerve center. We'll fry him up, Korean style."

FXs and Black Knights and Goodbye Weapons were formidable, but Billy thought about the stories he'd heard— Cthulhu taking down a satellite, or Cthulhu swallowing a nuke. He thought about what he had seen himself. That giant orca was still out there, so far as he knew. Those fish things, too. He realized that none of these measures had much of a chance of working, and at the same time, he realized that Plover and probably everyone else here already knew that, too. Perhaps that is what it was to be human—to fight on against overwhelming odds; to die in the noble struggle.

Or, maybe, they were just a bunch of jackasses. What had Maggie been talking about in the forest? Cthulhu as the inspiration for humanity. The fact that humans hearing *his* dreams was all that had allowed them to separate themselves from the beasts of the field. Could they be on the wrong side? Or was that the insanity working its way in?

"You alright, soldier?" a woman asked.

Billy nodded.

"Good. Plover wants you to go up there with him. Tell them about what you saw."

CHAPTER 28

He could sense it. It glowed in his mind, throbbing and beckoning with cold fingers. Wasp craved it with a lust more powerful than mere sexual lust; he wanted that stone, oh yes, and he knew his master wanted him to have it. Why else would it shine so brightly in his mind?

With the power of the piece of R'lyeh, he could heal his broken arm. He could unite the remaining humans and serve the Almighty Lord of the Sea. He could, in short, do anything he wanted.

He had spent the night sullenly drinking bourbon and bemoaning fate. All night long, waking or asleep, the rock of R'lyeh steadily grew in his head from faint spark to mighty beacon. A few hours after dawn, Wasp left the camp and smoldering fire on Mount Tabor with almost a hundred cultists in tow. There were too many people and not enough vehicles, so they rode in South American–style, two or three to a bike. Most were drunk, and all were heavily armed. It was, Wasp thought with grim satisfaction, a good old-fashioned American mob, the kind that marched on corrupt governors or toppled kings.

The trail led east. They stopped in a small suburb called Gresham, where several hundred additional bleary-eyed survivors joined them. Wasp guessed with an intuition not his own that the Dream phase of his master's plan was ending. People who had been sleeping for days or weeks were waking up. Something new was coming. Something big. Wasp couldn't fucking wait.

Ranks swelling and tanks full, they hit the highway and continued east. It wasn't easy, driving his bike with one hand, and the 84 was a bit rough, cracked and swollen from earthquakes. It remained passable, however, and many of the new members that had joined them were driving pickups and four-wheel drives.

It was cloudy but did not rain. He remembered and did not miss the endless gray autumn and winter days of Oregon. Visibility was bad enough that, until it was almost too late, they saw neither Mount Hood on their right nor the other mountain on their left. Wasp slowed, raising his good hand in the air to signify a group halt.

The one on their left was the Great Old One, Cthulhu, splashing his way up the Columbia River. *He* had just about reached the small town of Cascade Locks, and Wasp could sense that the Almighty One was aware of a threat—not scared but certainly mindful of it. Like knowing a bee is in the same room, or being coughed on by someone with the flu.

The stone was so seductively close that Wasp could feel his erection growing. But where? He sensed it was somewhere high up, on the God himself. The biker flipped up the visor of his helmet and swung his rifle up to use the scope.

The clouds remained, and it took a little bit of concentration, a little use of the small power his broken stone retained. What he saw shocked Wasp. He had to look again. Far up in the clouds, in the realm of alpine peaks and mountaintops, beneath the mass of squirming tentacles, was Powell's Bookstore. Or remnants of it, anyway; the roof was gone, half the building was gone, yet its iconic sign somehow remained. *What a waste of books*, he thought, and then had to laugh. Who needed dead trees with carbon runes on them anymore, anyway? The very idea of books suddenly seemed so ludicrous to him that he couldn't stop laughing.

"What do you see?" a young member of the Brotherhood asked him, as she peered up into the clouds. She could clearly see nothing.

"He moves in mysterious ways, friend."

He had hardly finished speaking when the planes appeared. More planes than he could count, all unloading devastation upon the Great Old One. The bookstore hurtled to the ground from several hundred feet up as Cthulhu's tentacles ripped planes from the air.

Leadership be damned. Wasp was on his bike, off-road, and zipping to the river within seconds. Which is why he didn't die when two planes appeared from the east and unloaded bombs upon the Brotherhood waiting behind him.

CHAPTER 29

Before they hit the water, several tentacles grabbed the building and lowered it gently into the river. Cold water rushed in with frigid enthusiasm. Any books that had not already fallen out were waterlogged and ruined. Maggie, Leonard, Cato, and Kamuks hit the wide river and swam with all their energy. Around them, smoking halves of planes crashed into the water. Once, somehow even more ominous, a severed tentacle splashed not far from them.

It was a long, tiring swim. The cold cramped Maggie's calf, but she was not going to give up now. At last, gasping, weary, and shivering, they reached a wooded shore on the Oregon side of the river. Just before them was a train track. A few hundred feet downstream were burnt-out cars.

High winds howled, and the trees bent from the force. Lining the shore about half a mile upriver were large, boxy tanks that fired missiles into Cthulhu. Above head, jets and drones fell from the sky like pollen on a spring day.

Something shiny caught Maggie's attention.

"What's that in your mouth, boy?" she asked. Kamuks turned his head from her. Before she could pursue it, Cato stood up.

"We have to run, now!" He had that strange disc in his hand. "These clouds are deadly." His voice cracked with abject terror; it was suffused with an instantly contagious fear that freaked her out.

Maggie looked up. The clouds glowed with an oozing green ichor. It was the least natural thing she had ever seen. It was the kind of natural disaster that might have ended the reign of the dinosaurs. She knew on a deep, instinctual level that getting hit by that rain could lead only to her own extinction.

The skies opened up; a deluge of cryptic poison poured forth.

"Run for the cars," Leonard said. He hobbled toward the remnants of the train. Maggie joined him, exhaustion replaced by adrenaline. Half a mile away, she saw a giant green claw slam down upon a mass of tanks. She saw no more as the four of them ducked into the closest train just as the fat green droplets sizzled their way down.

The car was missing a wall, and the front half of it had smashed into the train tracks. But the roof was still standing, and it provided protection from the ever-growing wind and the rain. The rain washed over the land, a poisonous monsoon, and the tall trees withered and shrank from its assault.

Maggie slumped in exhaustion next to her father. Kamuks walked in a circle three times then sat down, head on paws, facing the entrance. Cato sat across from them and tinkered with the strange item he carried. Something green stuck out of the water next to Cthulhu. Maggie stared for a few moments through the rain before she realized it was the remnants of the Bridge of the Gods.

A humming sound kept her from drifting off to sleep. She looked for the source, but even as her mind snapped back to reality, she realized what it was.

A motorcycle.

It was coming closer. Kamuks barked once and then, belying his age, jumped up and sideways as a bike crashed into the side of the door just two feet away from him. The dog's hackles raised, and he growled a low, warning growl.

A man wearing a motorcycle helmet strode in, holding a pistol in his good hand. Maggie knew at once who it was, even before he took off his helmet.

Wasp looked pretty rough. His arm remained awkwardly bandaged. Even though his helmet and leathers had kept him safe from the rain, his clothes were shrunken, sinking into him. "Give me the stone," he said, his voice urgent with need.

Maggie looked to Cato. Her eyes were wide with question.

"Give it to me," Wasp yelled.

"It's gone," Cato said, "fallen to the bottom of the river. Along with all those books."

"No, it isn't. It's here!" Wasp insisted. "I can sense it."

Maggie looked to her father, but his face was as blank as hers.

"I will shoot all of you!" Wasp shouted, full of junkie craving.

Kamuks opened his mouth to growl again. And something clattered to the ground.

CHAPTER 30

Wasp walked away from the shivering, huddled people and out into the rain. The stone was his. He clutched the strange angled piece of R'lyeh so tightly in his hand that he bled. But instead of hurting him, it energized him. The rain had become a soothing balm, a restorative tonic. His arm healed, and even aches and pains he had long since grown used to faded away. The high winds scarcely affected him. Wasp was imbued with power, and he raised his hands to the God that stood before him.

Cthulhu remained close to the ruins of the town of Cascade Locks. He was surrounded by planes and tanks and choppers and men with some sort of microwave batteries that radiated energy. Wasp had no doubt that if the US Army could get submarines into the Columbia River, they would. None of the attackers seemed to threaten the Almighty Lord of Time and Sea, but Wasp sensed that, collectively, they were actually frustrating their immortal opponent. A thought, as cold and ancient as time itself, reached into his head, swelling his brain:

DEFEND ME.

Wasp jumped onto his bike and drove back to the people he'd come with. In his single-minded rush to get the stone, he had neglected to think about them.

They were all dead, victims of a single plane cowardly dropping bombs from on high. Blackened corpses and burning, shattered wrecks of metal were all that was left. Anger at the imperialistic army assholes filled Wasp.

A many-tendriled daze spun his mind. It felt like taking DMT, the strangest mind-fuck he'd ever had. An ever-more-fluid sense of consciousness and the illusion of reality overwhelmed him. He has hyperaware, watching himself even as he acted.

Wasp saw himself stand on his bike and hold his hands out with a wide, sweeping motion. He raised one hand, quickly and dramatically, and tens of thousands of spores floated from the Great Old One and coated the burned corpses.

Wasp saw the dead rise, some barely more than animate

shadows, wraiths of eldritch wrath. Others had more substance, blackened and charred as they were. They climbed out of the wreckage of vehicles and assembled before him. Even death itself was no impediment for Cthulhu. *That is not dead which can eternal lie.*

Wasp's awareness was throbbing, and he soon was aware of another force approaching. Twisted sea creatures rose from the river and joined the dead cultists. They were loathsome fish men and clawed monstrosities, and they were there to serve him— Wasp, the high priest of Cthulhu.

He adjusted the bandana on his forehead as the devastatingly wonderful rain fell ever harder. And then he led the charge of the damned twenty miles up the road to root out and destroy the last of the US Army.

Wasp couldn't stop laughing, though it was only in his soul; his face remained grim and dour. He looped the stone on the cord around his neck. Life was so good he could taste it in the rain, see it in the bloody earth around him.

CHAPTER 31

Maggie watched Wasp stomp off into the rain. Whatever it was that he wanted, whatever her dog had held in his mouth, was no concern of hers. She was focused on surviving, on getting out of this situation, but it was too large, too overwhelming. She didn't even know where to begin.

"Can I see the Elder Sign?" Cato asked. "Just a piece."

She didn't want to part with it, but there was no harm. She reached into her bag. Her hand still ached from where it had been stabbed. She had lost track of days, but surely that hadn't happened more than a week ago. She handed two pieces of shattered and warped wood to the Norwegian.

Cato opened his strange device and pulled out tiny little discs.

"What are you doing?" Leonard asked him. His face was pale, and he looked old.

"It's just a guess. A wild hope. It would be easier if I had my glasses." He bent down and stared at the device with intense concentration. "According to one of the books I was reading, the Elder Sign is imbued with a kind of magic of the forgotten Old Ones. Space magic, maybe." He rubbed one of the pieces on the small discs. "Possibly I am attracting colonies of Otherspatial microbes, hostile to our big enemy out there. The Sign may even contain a chemical compound not found on earth."

"You really think it will work?" Maggie asked.

For the first time, he looked up. His eyes caught hers directly.

"Fuck, no," Cato said.

"It seemed like in the forest, you and Anna had a plan. Twelve-tone scales and geometry. Ring a bell?" Maggie said.

"She was the brilliant one," Cato said. "I have no doubt she could have come up with something overwhelmingly clever. All I can think of is shooting little pieces of Elder Sign at Cthulhu and hoping it doesn't piss him off too much."

"We don't have a lot of options at this point," Leonard said.

Maggie agreed. "So, do you think the Elder Sign can work in individual pieces?"

"In your dreams ..." Cato said. "If—"

Maggie's eyes got really big. "Of course. Why didn't I think of that?"

"Think of what?" Cato asked. Maggie barely heard him.

"Dad, remember when I was a little girl, and you would wake me up for hiking or fishing?"

He nodded uncertainly.

"Well, this is your chance to make up for it. Don't let anything wake me up."

He cocked his head, an unsure smile on his face.

"I mean it."

"Alright, I got it."

"You, too," she said to Cato. He seemed less confused than her father. He had perhaps guessed her intentions.

"No matter what," Cato said.

Maggie lay down on the hard train floor, resting her head on Kamuks, and surrendered to the pressure of the dreams.

***

Maggie is her dream. Her dream is Maggie. Strange days are here again, she thinks. In her hand, the Elder Sign is whole once more. She cries with previously suppressed emotion and long-held fear. SHIFT Cthulhu stands before her, no longer indistinct or incomprehensible. She sees him for what he truly is: an ancient, lonely being trapped in a land far from home. SHIFT Cthulhu takes notice of her. Tentacles slither toward her but are rebuffed by the Elder Sign. SHIFT An army of man-sized Cthulhu-like creatures appear around her. SHIFT She is alone, without friends, and the spawn of the Great Old One are pressing in on her. SHIFT There are too many, and though she destroys a dozen, a score, she is pressed to the earth and crushed. She scarcely feels it. Her gaze is held fast by the giant. SHIFT Claws piercing her. SHIFT Tentacles choking her. SHIFT Darkness.

CHAPTER 32

Across the galaxy, two immense beings of eternal power watch with fervid interest.

"*She is brave*," said the first.

"She is foolish."

"*Often the same thing, for these creatures.*"

"Brave or foolish, this one will die," replied the second. **"Seems to be her fate."**

"*That cannot be,*" said the first entity. "*She carries our sign. She knows what it is. We have turned from the universes that she died once already.*"

"True that it is unwise to give up on her now, when she is so close," said the second. **"Perhaps we can send her the fools."**

"*Interesting. One of them did consecrate his death to us. Y'nghai.*"

"Not surprising, considering where he's been," said the second. **"What he's done."**

"*How much of that can he remember?*" the first one asked.

"The human subconscious is an impressive piece of construction. The Tentacled One has had millions of years to perfect it."

"*He is not entirely with fault, I begrudgingly admit. We are in agreement then?*"

"It is in our power. And it is far more amusing to thwart our opponent this way."

"*Let them return,*" the first said. "*And fill the dreams with brave foolishness.*"

It was no sooner said than done, and both Elder Things watched in hungry anticipation.

CHAPTER 33

The remaining soldiers were no pushovers, he had to admit. Confronted by a force of insubstantial shadow zombies and monsters from the sea, they had taken out a lot of his warriors on their way to the town of Hood River. The army had missiles and bombs and mines and drones—all the technology in the world— but in the end, they had no answer for the sheer eldritch power of their opponents.

Wasp clutched his hands together and concentrated. Dark purple lightning cracked down from the sky. The people it hit instantly mutated into gibbering, squamous monstrosities. Seeing their friends warp into scaly, teeth-gnashing beasts was too much, and most of those "spared" ran, only to be caught and killed by pursuing fish men.

A few took shelter in one of the large breweries. No doubt they called for and were waiting for support, but Wasp knew the last of the planes and tanks were even now being crushed by Cthulhu. He could sense that, but even with all of the threats soon to be eliminated, the Great Old One remained troubled. Wasp hoped that by killing the last of the resistance his master would be free of all worries.

He ordered the remaining cultists, the scorched, stuttering souls, to advance into the brewery. They surged in through broken windows and smashed the door down. There were booming gunshots, and then Wasp frowned. He no longer had any impression whatsoever of his stygian servants. He shook his head in disappointment. "If you want to do something wrong, you have to do it yourself," he said. He jumped off his bike and—

Two soldiers shot him in the head before the shambles of the door. One of his arms morphed into a tentacle and smacked them down with divine speed.

"Motherfucker!" he heard a woman curse.

"Better run, hombres!" Wasp shouted. "Last chance before I kill you."

Another bullet whizzed at him; it too was batted down by his tentacle, causing him no harm. The tentacle struck him as much cooler than his former boring human hand.

It was too easy to find and crush the soldiers. Their bullets could not harm him. One by one, he hunted them down and smashed or choked them with his tentacle. Before long, it seemed everyone was dead. He found the last man, a gray-haired stern man that looked like a general, hiding behind the bar in the main room. He had been the most fun to kill. Wasp had squeezed his neck so hard that one of his eyes popped out.

Wasp poured himself a celebratory pint, drank it, and turned to leave. A long-haired figure he'd somehow missed, a man with gaping pits for eyes, stood before him. A shotgun pointed at Wasp's chest. The blind man didn't hesitate. He blasted the automatic shotgun at Wasp from point-blank range.

The biker's hand tentacle blurred to catch the shells, but even his blasphemous power couldn't block them all. Three shots hit Wasp. Two in the chest, though they healed instantly. But one hit him in the stone, the rock of R'lyeh, hanging around his neck.

Wasp went flying back. He landed hard on his back, but it saved his life. The blind soldier shot again, but too high, and the shells missed. The high priest of Cthulhu reached into his pocket and pulled out his pistol. "You punkass blindass motherfucker," he growled, and he emptied the clip into his enemy. The man grunted, and his mouth opened in surprise before he slumped to the ground. Blood pooled around him from the multiple bullet wounds.

Wasp sat up, reached for his rock, and screamed. The stone was shattered. His link to the master was severed. He was, more or less, human again, though his left hand remained a tentacle.

Wasp stormed out of the brewery, stopping only to kick the dead man in the ribs as hard as he could on the way out.

CHAPTER 34

SHIFT

Maggie lay gasping on the river's shore. A great weight lifted from her, and she could breathe again. Pieces of the Cthulhu spawn lay all about her. Two warriors dressed like Arthurian knights, holding laser swords instead of metal blades, flanked her. Their swords dripped yellow bile.

"Fear not, maiden. Your warriors have returned to battle with thee," said the taller one.

"For thee," the other said.

"Aye, verily," said the first one amiably. "For thee." His voice was muffled by the helmet, but Maggie knew in a flash who they were.

"Orson? Arlo?"

"At your service, my lady," Arlo bowed, even as Orson flipped his visor up.

"If by my life or death I can protect you, I will," Orson said.

"Am I dead then?"

Arlo shrugged. "Isn't dying just a really long dream?"

"I was never really sure about the metaphysics of it all," Orson said. "What I am sure of is that we are here to help you."

"Help me what?"

"Kill Cthulhu, of course," Arlo said.

"He can be killed?" she asked.

"Oh, no. Not by us, anyway."

"Excuse me?"

The wind began to howl.

SHIFT The three warriors of the Dreamlands fought their way through nightmares unimaginable. The Elder Sign was a match for all the horrors the Dreaming God could summon. Sheer numbers no longer overwhelmed the maiden, as the two dream swordsmen were avatars of war and battle.

SHIFT

The two warriors, their armor dinged and bloody, explained to her, on the precipice of a volcano filled with shadowy hands that reached for them, that Cthulhu could not be killed, but that if they hurt him enough, he would return home.

"Home?" she asked.

"Home to R'lyeh," Orson said. "The land of dreams."

"Think of it as a when, and not a where," Arlo said.

"How do you know these things?" she asked.

"How do you not?" Orson said. SHIFT

***

A skinny man in skinny jeans, his lank blond hair greasy with sweat and filth, stood on the beach. In his hand was a toy, a joke. He raised the rounded weapon and quite solemnly fired it into the Great Old One.

***

The Elder Sign blazed with sanctified fury, lighting up the bottom of the sea. Arlo remained at Maggie's side, but she was not sure when Orson had left, or what had happened to him. An image of teeth was all she could recall. The bodies of dead sea creatures floated. SHIFT

She strode into an ancient city where the very architecture made her uneasy. It was empty. After much exploration, Arlo cried out as a wizened and small creature scuttled away. She chased it down and smote it with the Elder Sign. Long tentacles reached for her as an undulating cry … SHIFT

The wind blasted her, and she was vaguely aware it had broken Arlo into little pieces, had distributed his essence in a million different places. The same thing was perhaps happening to her, and she could not summon … SHIFT

***

Tentacles and fish men and burnt cultist corpses alike reached for the thin man on the beach. But his gun blazed, mowed them down with inescapable force. Still, he sensed that even with fragments of the Elder Sign in the gun and strapped to it, he was merely annoying his titanic opponent.

Annoyance was a major step up, however. And it bought Maggie more time for whatever she was going to do.

The Ragnarök sputtered to a halt. Cato had run out of ammo.

Tentacles crawled from the river, and a squamous hand reached for him.

***

Everything was gone. Maggie stood on the Bridge of the Gods

once more. She was alone. She closed her eyes and breathed deeply. *Goodbye, Kamuks*, she thought.

A warm hand cradled her face. It felt shockingly intimate, and her eyes—her Self—snapped open. She stood, jolted awake; she found herself on some vast rubbery hill. The river below her was black and full of snakes. There was no sign of the ruined trains where her father hid.

Billy Crow cupped her face with his long brown hands. He stared at her with beautiful brown eyes.

"Your eyes," she said. "You're healed. You're safe."

"*Awake, arise, or be for ever fall'n.*" Crow said. His voice was a weary, sad, and tremulant whisper. As Maggie watched, his body blew away, disintegrating into a thousand motes of light and spirit and love.

"Goodbye," Maggie shouted into the wind. "Goodbye!" There was so much more she wanted to say—had to say—not only to Billy, but to Orson and Arlo and her mother and to every loved one she had ever lost, but words failed her. Tears filled her eyes but did not fall.

***

She sat up, gasping. Her father snored gently beside her, but Cato and her dog were gone. She was awake, alive, and alone.

CHAPTER 35

Maggie wandered out of the wrecked train. It was not raining at all anymore, and the evening sky was clear of all clouds. The air seemed fresh and cool and, for the first time in a long time, free of the tainted, spectral atmosphere.

Cato stood down at the waterfront. When he saw her, he dropped the gun in his hand and rushed to her. His footsteps ground into the gravel, and he caught her in a massive hug, lifting her from her feet.

"He's gone! We've done it!"

"Put me down," Maggie said. But his words were only beginning to sink in. She felt like she had been asleep for years. "He's dead? We did it?"

"Not truly dead, I guess," Cato said. "But look." He pointed at the river. The mass that had been tentacles and wings and teeth and legs and claws had melted into a pile of matter that stretched from Portland to Washington.

"That's him?" she asked.

"That's his shell. His essence fled. My bullets hurt him, I think, but something else defeated him. One moment he was mighty and terrible and wrathful, and the next? He just sort of deflated." Cato gripped her wrists. "Maggie, what did you do?"

She broke free of his grasp and shook her head. In her dreams lurked a nameless sadness. But something caught her attention. There was a shirtless man in the water. He was far away and the light was dim, but Maggie thought he looked familiar.

"Look," Cato said. "Cthulhu fell where that old bridge was. His body stretches from shore to shore."

"The Bridge of the Sea God," Maggie muttered.

"I like it," Cato said. "If anyone is still around to ever use it."

"What's happened in the rest of the world?" she asked.

Cato held his hands up helplessly. "I wish I knew. We need to find out."

"Portland is utterly destroyed," she said. The price of survival was only now making itself clear. "It's a town of ruins and stumps. Everyone I know has to be dead."

"Look up," Cato said. The first stars were visible in the night sky. They were not dancing, or in new, loathsome formations. The stars were once again simply *right*.

"It's true then," Maggie said. "We won."

"He doesn't think so," Cato said, pointing to the man in the water. The shirtless man noticed their attention and waded out of the cold water toward them.

It didn't take long for him to reach them. Wasp climbed out of the water. One of his hands was gone, and in its place was a four-foot-long tentacle.

"You've done it," he said. His tone was as bitter as the blackest coffee. "You've killed God."

"Maybe we can see what humans can do without help," Maggie said.

"That reminds me," Cato said. He picked up a large rock and carried it over to his gun, where he drove it down, again and again, until the thing was a smoking wreck. He then flung the thing out into the river.

"Your arm is a tentacle," Maggie said to Wasp, while they watched the Norwegian scientist destroy the world's deadliest weapon.

"Yeah, well, it's not all bad. I always was kind of a weirdo."

"Somehow I don't think that's what they meant by 'Keep Portland Weird,'" she said.

Wasp didn't smile. "Heard that one before."

EPILOGUE

Far, far across the lengths of space, time, and other dimensions, the pair of Elder Gods are delighted. They have won their game, a game they have played since before the beginning of time, since before the beginning of beginnings. They don't always win, but they always expect to.

"The guardian is dead. Gh"ll Gnh'gua."

"He's not dead. He's simply fled back several million years in time."

"Much the same."

"Ph'nglui. Yes, much the same."

"The planet shall be ours."

"For a sweet moment, yes. And then after it's destroyed? Where to next?"

"That is always the interesting question, isn't it?"

SEVERED**PRESS**

f facebook.com/severedpress
twitter.com/severedpress

CHECK OUT OTHER GREAT KAIJU NOVELS

KAIJU WINTER
by Jake Bible

The Yellowstone super volcano has begun to erupt, sending North America into chaos and the rest of the world into panic. People are dangerous and desperate to escape the oncoming mega-eruption, knowing it will plunge the continent, and the world, into a perpetual ashen winter. But no matter how ready humanity is, nothing can prepare them for what comes out of the ash: Kaiju!

RAIJU
by K.H. Koehler

His home destroyed by a rampaging kaiju, Kevin Takahashi and his father relocate to New York City where Kevin hopes the nightmare is over. Soon after his arrival in the Big Apple, a new kaiju emerges. Qilin is so powerful that even the U.S. Military may be unable to contain or destroy the monster. But Kevin is more than a ragged refugee from the now defunct city of San Francisco. He's also a Keeper who can summon ancient, demonic god-beasts to do battle for him, and his creature to call is Raiju, the oldest of the ancient Kami. Kevin has only a short time to save the city of New York. Because Raiju and Qilin are about to clash, and after the dust settles, there may be no home left for any of them!

CHECK OUT OTHER GREAT KAIJU NOVELS

MURDER WORLD ǀ KAIJU DAWN
by Jason Cordova & Eric S Brown

Captain Vincente Huerta and the crew of the Fancy have been hired to retrieve a valuable item from a downed research vessel at the edge of the enemy's space.
It was going to be an easy payday.
But what Captain Huerta and the men, women and alien under his command didn't know was that they were being sent to the most dangerous planet in the galaxy.
Something large, ancient and most assuredly evil resides on the planet of Gorgon IV. Something so terrifying that man could barely fathom it with his puny mind. Captain Huerta must use every trick in the book, and possibly write an entirely new one, if he wants to escape Murder World.

KAIJU ARMAGEDDON
by Eric S. Brown

The attacks began without warning. Civilian and Military vessels alike simply vanished upon the waves. Crypto-zoologist Jerry Bryson found himself swept up into the chaos as the world discovered that the legendary beasts known as Kaiju are very real. Armies of the great beasts arose from the oceans and burrowed their way free of the Earth to declare war upon mankind. Now Dr. Bryson may be the human race's last hope in stopping the Kaiju from bringing civilization to its knees.
This is not some far distant future. This is not some alien world. This is the Earth, here and now, as we know it today, faced with the greatest threat its ever known. The Kaiju Armageddon has begun.

CHECK OUT OTHER GREAT KAIJU NOVELS

ATOMIC REX
by Matthew Dennion

The war is over, humanity has lost, and the Kaiju rule the earth.

Three years have passed since the US government attempted to use giant mechs to fight off an incursion of kaiju. The eight most powerful kaiju have carved up North America into their respective territories and their mutant offspring also roam the continent. The remnants of humanity are gathered in a remote settlement with Steel Samurai, the last of the remaining mechs, as their only protection. The mech is piloted by Captain Chris Myers who realizes that humanity will not survive if they stay at the settlement. In order to preserve the human race, he leaves the settlement unprotected as he engages on a desperate plan to draw the eight kaiju into each other's territories. His hope is that the kaiju will destroy each other. Chris will encounter horrors including the amorphous Amebos, Tortiraus the Giant turtle , and the nuclear powered mutant dinosaur Atomic Rex!

KAIJU DEADFALL
by JE Gurley

Death from space. The first meteor landed in the Pacific Ocean near San Francisco, causing an earthquake and a tsunami. The second wiped out a small Indiana city. The third struck the deserts of Nevada. When gigantic monsters- Ishom, Girra, and Nusku- emerge from the impact craters, the world faces a threat unlike any it had ever known - Kaiju . NASA catastrophist Gate Rutherford and Special Ops Captain Aiden Walker must find a way to stop the creatures before they destroy every major city in America..

CHECK OUT OTHER GREAT KAIJU NOVELS

KAIJU SPAWN
by David Robbins
& Eric S Brown

Wally didn't believe it was really the end of the world until he saw the Kaiju with his own eyes. The great beasts rose from the Earth's oceans, laying waste to civilization. Now Wally must fight his way across the Kaiju ravaged wasteland of modern day America in search of his daughter. He is the only hope she has left . . . and the clock is ticking.

From authors David Robbins (Endworld) and Eric S Brown (Kaiju Apocalypse), Kaiju Spawn is an action packed, horror tale of desperate determination and the battle to overcome impossible odds.

KUA MAU
by Mark Onspaugh

The Spider Islands. A mysterious ship has completed a treacherous journey to this hidden island chain. Their mission: to capture the legendary monster, Kua'Mau. Thinking they are successful, they sail back to the United States, where the terrifying creature will be displayed at a new luxury casino in Las Vegas. But the crew has made a horrible mistake - they did not trap Kua'Mau, they took her offspring. Now hot on their heels comes a living nightmare, a two hundred foot, one hundred ton tentacled horror, Kua'Mau, Kaiju Mother of Wrath, who will stop at nothing to safeguard her young. As she tears across California heading towards Vegas, she leaves a monumental body-count in her wake, and not even the U.S. military or private black ops can stop this city-crushing, havoc-wreaking monstrous mother of all Kaiju as she seeks her revenge.

www.ingramcontent.com/pod-product-compliance
Lightning Source LLC
Chambersburg PA
CBHW051945170626
46808CB00007B/2483